The Protestant Catholic

Contents:

This book is dedicated to all those who grew up in the Northern Ireland 'Troubles' and who like me, have had to live with the mental scars and still maintain normal lives.

Roy McCartney

Foreword/Introduction:

This book is really a compilation of stories of my growing up in Belfast in the troubled 70s and 80s. It is about 90 per cent biographical, with all the names changed to protect the real people involved. I was brought up a Catholic from a Protestant Father and a Catholic Mother (mixed marriage) and I found this conflicted with all my feelings, hopes and passions. I was always a Unionist in my family traditions and politics, yet because of the religious conflict in Northern Ireland, I was mistrusted and often badly treated by both sides. I spent my young life constantly trying to prove my pride in being British, while at the same time resenting the intense Irish Nationalism that I believed nearly destroyed the country of my birth.

In more recent years, as a teacher in the North of England, I realised my stories were intriguing to my students, who never had to grow up in a war-torn land of discrimination and murder. Thankfully, I was able to keep clear of the worst of the Troubles, by not joining any politically active organisations and perhaps also, by working in the Imperial Civil Service. There are some horrific events and aspects that I could not relate in my book, due to the fact that they were covered widely in the press at the time and I am not wanting to open up old wounds or upset any of my readers. This book is intended to give an insight into how it felt as a

child and young person, growing up in a land where hated and mistrust was rife and how living with fear of death and serious injury was a daily routine. I hope it will prove an interesting and intriguing read.

Roy McCartney

The Protestant Catholic

By Roy McCartney

Chapter 1:

The Parents

Alan McCree was staring. He didn't take his eyes of the skinny brunette on the Plaza dance floor. His friend Joe was muttering impatiently and grabbing at his arm. 'Will you come on Alan, she's just another bloody fenian, you've been staring at her all friggin' night!' The bar had just closed, so Alan and Joe headed in the direction of the door. They hesitated in the hallway, as it was a typical wet and chilly Belfast evening and they both needed to prepare themselves against the elements. 'Yeah, come on Joe' he suddenly replied thoughtfully, 'I'm not looking forward to walking all the way back up Sandy Row, in this bloody weather. Have you seen the rain? It's pishin' it down!' Joe continued, 'Look Alan, I know you have been dancing with this girl quite a lot recently and that's so great, but that is a totally different thing to asking her out on a proper date. Just be careful!' Joe warned. Alan answered 'Joe, thanks but look, I really don't give a damn about all the religious differences crap! She's a cracking, very attractive girl and a bloody great dancer. I know she is engaged, but have you seen the state of that stupid fiance of hers. He has absolutely no interest in her dancing and anyway, I heard he might be becoming a priest instead of getting married to her. He's a proper, 'lick the altar' rails Fenian and he apparently thinks dancing is a sin …Oh and I'm told he goes to chapel about six times a week and everything!' Joe just gave him a despairing look 'How do you know all this shit about her? I hope you know what the hell you are doing! Anyway, she might not want to go out with a 'Proddy' milkman from Sandy Row?... Now can we please just head home? I would love to get out of this horrible, shitty rain?'

The following Saturday evening, Alan went on his own to Belfast's favourite, Plaza dance hall. Joe had other things to do and just decided to leave him to get on with his plans. Sure enough, the subject of his interest was there, dancing the night away with her usual group of friends. He waited for the right opportunity and then approached her respectfully, asking very eloquently, but with a slight element of humour. 'Ah… hi Jeanette, can I please have the honour of this foxtrot with you?' She smiled teasingly, didn't speak and then suddenly grabbed Alan's hand, sweeping them both onto the dance floor. Throughout the evening Alan kept coming over from his seat near the bar, to get Jeanette onto the floor. She observed 'Um…You seem to be on your own tonight, Alan. It's just that my friends have noticed! You do know that I am engaged to someone, don't you?' Alan shrugged and mockingly replied 'Yeah! to that nutter who wants to be a priest. I heard all about him. He doesn't come to dancing 'coz he's too bloody holy! What do you see in the ijit anyway?' She glared at him in mild disapproval, but before she could answer, Alan quickly chipped in with 'Oh, and can I give you a lift home tonight, by the way. I've got my lovely Morgan three-wheeler parked just around the corner, in Shaftesbury Square?'

'Well, you must be doing alright Alan McCree! You have your own car eh? ...Yeah, I guess you can take me home!' Jeanette replied thoughtfully. 'I'll just have to make sure that the girls are okay about going home without me! They will probably prefer to walk anyway!'

Once they were in the car, Alan keenly asked if they could be dance partners and even do some ballroom competitions together. It was possible to win a few pounds, in those days and they were both competitive minded people. He explained that he really admired her dancing ability and that they would make a formidable team. 'I'll think about it, Goodnight Alan!' Jeanette replied, as she slammed the car door.

Jeanette's Aunt Agnes heard her coming in the back door of their tiny kitchen house. She was sitting nervously on a stool near the stairs. 'It's way past midnight, where the hell have you been? Was that Christopher? I didn't know he had a car!' Jeanette glared at her over-protective inquisitor. 'No actually Aunt Agnes, his name is Alan and we have been dancing together quite a lot, at the Plaza ballroom. He is a very genuine guy and is great at the foxtrot and quick step!... Oh... and he's a protestant, before you say anything; and I really like him!' Aunt Agnes digested this information for a moment, frowned and then turned her back with an air of despairing resignation. 'Good night, Jeanette, glad you are back safe' she muttered, shaking her head as she wandered back to bed.

The next few Saturdays saw Alan and Jeanette steadily strengthen their bond of friendship and develop their ballroom skills together, as a dance couple. They even felt confident enough to enter several dancing competitions together, as they had planned. This later led to a few second and third places. The Plaza had some excellent dancers from all over Northern Ireland. They both enjoyed it and made a few quid, but they knew they weren't ever going to set the world alight.

Jeanette found out from a conversation with one of her girlfriends that her fiancé Christopher had been regularly going out drinking with his mates, even though he had told her that they must both stay in, as they were meant to be saving for an as yet unspecified wedding date. Jeanette realised her feelings were becoming very strong for Alan and he had already told her the same. She decided to confront Christopher, the next time they met. Christopher listened to her intently as she pointed out the problems in their relationship and he didn't argue or disagree with anything she said. Then after a thoughtful pause he uttered 'Actually, I am having serious second thoughts about the whole marriage thing. My mother and I have been talking about everything and we agreed that I should go to St. Joseph's Seminary and train for the priesthood instead of getting married!' It was now apparent that Alan's suspicions about him had been right, all along. Jeanette glared back at Christopher, totally bewildered, but feeling relieved at the same time.

'I'm so glad that is settled, she finally replied, sarcastically. 'You have led me a merry dance for months Christopher and

I have to admit, I was getting a bit sick of trying to compete with your darling mother for your affections. Believe it or not, this guy I met at dancing is just the right kind of man for me and guess what?... He is a protestant and unlike you, he is a totally honest human being! In fact, the more I think about it Christopher, you will be a perfect candidate for the priesthood!' Jeanette eased a small gold and sapphire ring off her finger, as she spoke. She unfurled Christopher's fingers and gently placed it into his palm, at which point she smiled bemusedly towards the ground, turned away and started to walk towards the bus stop. 'Bye, Christopher; have a nice life!' He shrugged his shoulders and held his hands up in dismay, then he slowly moved back along the street. 'What else did he expect?' Jeanette thought quietly to herself.

Jeanette and Alan soon realised that neither of their families would be too pleased with them, for finding a partner on the other side of the religious divide. Over the next few months Jeanette's Catholic family started to realise that she really loved Alan and after many discussions around the family table, they gradually came to accept him. The reason may have been partly because her father was an ex-British soldier with the Blues and Royals and all five of her brothers, had served with the British forces, mostly during World war two. They certainly were not a Nationalist family, like the vast majority of Falls Road Catholics. The inference here being that the 'Jeanette having a Protestant boyfriend' thing, wasn't such a big deal to any of them.

The complete opposite could be said of Alan's family. They were an absolute nightmare. Although they were all

Protestant, they went to different churches. One was a Methodist, then there were two of Alan's brothers, who were presbyterian and his oldest sister was a member of the Congregational church. Alan and his father and Mother were all Church of Ireland. Several other members of his larger extended family attended other less well-known denominations of the Protestant faith. Every one of them ate up bible passages each day with scary fanaticism! Belfast was full of options for anyone looking for a choice of versions of Protestantism. Apparently, when they were all together, they could spend hours fighting and arguing about interpretations of just about every aspect of the bible. Jesus himself would have found it all hilarious!

In the coming months, they collectively behaved disgracefully and very unchristian-like towards Jeanette, often referring to her as a Fenian and a useless Papist! She was not made welcome at all for the first two years of their relationship. In the end just a few of Alan's family members seemed to accept her and this was only in a lukewarm manner, when Alan finally announced they were getting married.

The most difficult family member was always going to be Alan's Dad. Robert McCree was a staunch Orangeman. He had pictures of King Billy crossing the Boyne, in three different rooms in the house and on a huge metal plaque on the wall of the outdoor toilet. To him, one of his sons marrying a 'Fenian', was totally inconceivable. It didn't matter that she was the daughter of a family with strong British army traditions. She was a papist!

The local Protestant churches didn't want to know about staging their wedding, as it was 1957 and Catholics were just Jacobites and Fenians and not to be tolerated or trusted in any way. Jeanette, being a good Catholic girl, decided she should go to St. Peter's Catholic Pro cathedral on the Falls Road, to consult with the Parish priest, Canon Locke and get his Ecumenical advice. He was helpful and sympathetic up to a point, but he said that the Catholic Church would only consider this marriage, if Alan studied the Catechism (the Catholic religious protocol manual of the day) and was baptised a Catholic. Alan clearly could never agree to this in principle or practicality and after Jeanette cajoled him into a lengthy meeting with the Canon himself, it was eventually agreed that he would let any children from the marriage, be brought up as Catholics, but he himself would retain his personal religious status as a Church of Ireland member. The Canon had a younger cousin, who was a parish priest based in Kensington in London, and he said he would be only too happy to perform the marriage ceremony there. 'Wait a minute', squirmed Alan, 'Why London?' 'Because, my son' said a patronising Canon Locke… 'This is Belfast and we cannot set a precedent, by letting a Protestant marry one of our daughters on Irish soil. It's just not how we do things!' Within a few days Jeanette's Aunt Agnes rang Jeanette's older brother Patrick, who lived and worked in Kensington and explained the situation to him. This small-minded religious nonsense was one of the reasons he had left Northern Ireland, in the first place. Agnes gave him all the relevant details of the Canon's cousin's church, which was situated very close to where Patrick lived and he dutifully arranged the marriage for the Saturday two weeks hence. Jeanette and Alan very quickly organised the boat and train trip to London and with the help of Patrick's family, were married in a quiet ceremony in London on 31st May 1957. Jeanette remembered that Aunt Agnes never messed about when things needed done.

Initially, Robert McCree refused to allow his son back under his roof after the marriage. He couldn't hide his contempt for 'Taigs! and would not break with Orange tradition. He certainly did not want to allow Jeanette in his house. It was months before he eventually agreed to let Alan and Jeanette across his door and even then, he didn't congratulate them on their marriage. Jeanette's aunt Agnes was completely the opposite and quite happily accommodated the newlyweds for several months, while Alan searched for somewhere suitable to live. Jeanette had lived with her aunt since she was about four years old, as her mother was 47 years old when she gave birth to her and simply could not be bothered bringing up another child after 8 much older siblings. In those days, the Catholic church were totally against any form of contraception. This allowed drunken, horny husbands to have their wicked way on a Saturday night, after an evening in the pub and for wives to take the life changing consequences nine months later! A lot of Belfast babies were created in this way, in those days. Jeanette was sadly perpetually aware, that her genetic mother thought of her as just an accident!

Alan eventually found a little housing estate called Rushpark, just north of Belfast, for him to properly house his new family and they moved into a two-bedroom flat by the end of that year. Rushpark was still a new estate and they were developing an even bigger estate, Rathcoole, right next door. This was becoming an exciting start for Alan and Jeanette as an unlikely couple, even though Jeanette felt surrounded by suspicious and wary protestants. She just had to be discreet about her church going and often used to sneak out to Whitehouse Catholic church, early on Sunday mornings. Locally, anyone who went to the Catholic church was said to be 'going to Chapel'! In the late fifties and early sixties, the Catholic Mass was still in Latin and it seemed to give most Protestants a feeling that it was all a bit strange and creepy. The main difference was the Transubstantiation, where Catholics believed that communion really was the body and blood of Christ (in its' most Spiritual perception), whereas Protestants believed it was simply a reverential celebration and re-enactment of the events of the Last Supper. In truth, the hatred and mistrust between Catholics and Protestants was really a political one and it still is today. It was always more about the 'Boyne' in 1690, British Rule in Ireland and about the geographical divisions brought about by the creation of the Irish 'Free State' in 1922. No matter where you went in Northern Ireland, someone always asked you what school you went to. Unless you told a blatant lie, they could tell straight away, if you were a Protestant or a Catholic. There weren't any mixed religion schools in Belfast back then and that is largely still the case today, with just a few exceptions.

Chapter 2:

Billy the Kid

Jeanette gave birth to a son on 12th March 1958. William Robert McCree, was named after both of his of his grandfathers, but he just became known as 'Billy'. A year later, he had a baby sister Anne and so the family had no choice but to move to one of the bigger houses in Rathcoole. Alan left his milk delivery job and instead he drove a large mobile crane, putting up lamp posts all over Belfast, for the Northern Ireland Electricity board. It was much better paid and in the next few years the addition of two more children Joseph and Agnes, meant that he also had to acquire an evening job as an ice cream vendor, working for his brother-in-law, in order to afford to feed all six of them. Alan used to proudly boast about selling ice cream to football legend George Best, whose parents lived on his route in the Cregagh area of Belfast. He was apparently a regular customer, often signing autographs for kids, as he stood in the ice cream queue at Alan's van.

Billy's early years were quite uneventful, but he started to realise from about 4 years old that the society he was born into was a very factionalised one. Both Alan and Jeanette were constantly telling him what he was or was not allowed to say and do, depending on which grandparent or relative he was visiting. He was often told, as he got older 'Watch your mouth, don't talk politics, don't say anything controversial or better still, just keep your flamin' gob shut!' He usually did!

One of the earliest memories Billy had, was when Alan's motorbike caught fire, shortly after they had moved to Rathcoole. He was about 3 years old, but distinctly remembered Alan had hand-built a sturdy two-seater sidecar onto his bike, and Jeanette was sitting in it with baby Anne on her knee. Billy had just sat down in the small rear seat, when suddenly flames started to shoot out of the engine of the old BSA Norton 500. They had been just about to drive off to visit Jeanette's mum (Granny Cameron), when everything started to happen very quickly. Jeanette ordered Billy out of the back seat and she handed Anne to him. She leapt out of the sidecar and got the three of them a safe distance from the bike. In the meantime, Alan had obtained a bucket from a neighbour, who just happened to be working in his garden and filled it with sand from a nearby building site, down the street. He threw the sand over the engine, to put the fire out, as water would have wrecked the engine completely. It was a lucky escape for them all, as it could have been a tragedy. Alan drove Jeanette mad for most of the next week, as he completely took the motorbike apart. He did most of this inside the house, covering everywhere in oil and sand from the dousing of the flames. He then slowly reassembled it all again in the backyard. The engine had to have the sand hoovered out of it and then be repaired, as the fire had taken its' toll. The cause was a fractured fuel line from the petrol tank, that had leaked petrol all over the engine. They were so lucky it hadn't exploded. Alan saw this as a challenge and fixed it all himself, as his determination and instinctive engineering skills came to good use.

Over the next few years, young Billy had to endure getting punched and kicked and called a Fenian and a Taig bastard, by kids who knew that he didn't go to their school and since he passed them, going the opposite way in the mornings, they realised he had to be going to the Catholic, Stella Maris Primary school at the top end of the estate. Billy used to hear them muttering as they walked past, 'He must be 'one of them!' or 'his eyes are too close together, I bet he is a fucking Taig'! It was scary and he used to think to himself, 'Do Catholics really have eyes that are closer together than Protestants?' Jeanette had to frequently visit the school to complain about the staff not keeping the kids safe from name calling, stone throwing and beatings, outside the school. Then to make matters even worse, the kids from the Nationalist Bawnmore estate, who also attended Billy's school, started beating him up because in their eyes he was a 'Snout' and a 'Proddy lover'! Billy was becoming an early victim of both sides in the underlying religious intolerance, that eventually erupted in the start of 'The Troubles' in 1969.

In 1960s Rathcoole, kids were very resourceful at making their own entertainment. They often played 'kerbsy' with a football in the main street, or they picked teams and played a version of 'Hunts' or 'Rally-O', which involved one team collectively catching the other, with the entire Housing estate as the gaming area. It involved a lot of running, as Rathcoole was the biggest housing estate in Britain around that time.

When Billy was 7 years old, he got a Zorro costume from Santa. The previous year, he had got a large red and white tricycle. They still hadn't finished the road surface near the

Baptist Church at the end of his street and so there was a deep indent in the road, allowing it to fill up to about two feet deep with water when it rained. The resulting large puddle was at the bottom of a steep hill and attracted the local kids like a small paddling pool. Our hero decided that he was going to soak the other kids playing at this occasional pool, by riding his trike through the water at speed. Picture little Billy shooting down the hill on his trike, with his Zorro mask on and his black cape flying in the wind. The wave caused by his impact through the water was devastating to the other little kids, but he did completely soak himself in the process. After about 3 of these Sorties, he decided to go home. When he got there the other kids mums' were queueing at the door to complain about him soaking their little darlings. Once inside, Jeanette battered him with his Dad's belt, as parents did in the 1960s and then dumped his sobbing naked body in the bath, while she put his saturated clothes into the Burco boiler to wash. Very few people had a proper washing machine, back then. The problem with the Burco boiler, was that clothes often shrank with the excessive heat. Subsequently, The Zorro suit was quite a bit smaller the next time Billy wore it, with the trouser legs a few inches short of his ankles!

Older pre-teens used to love building their own Go Karts out of planks of wood, with pram wheels at the front and always ball bearing-wheels at the back. The plank that was used for the body, had a whole drilled near the front with a huge bolt through it and a smaller cross plank, on which the pram wheels were attached, usually the axle support was a row of long and carefully bent nails, or some large hooks, if they were available. Then a strong rope or cord was attached to each end of the small plank to create a steering control. They were held together with more nails and bent hooks and anything else that could be improvised to strengthen the final product. The ball bearing wheels were usually set on the end of a carved length of wood, as a rear axle and nailed securely into place. The result of all this, was a queue of noisy, nutty kids at the top of the hilly streets of Owenreagh Drive and East Way, all dying to try out their newly built 'Guiders' (as they were called) for speed and control on the slopes. The noise from the metal ball bearing wheels was horrendous and echoed around that entire part of the estate. No one ever thought of adding brakes and so there were often grazed arms and legs and even a few cut heads, at the end of the day. The favourite mode for braking, was the side of one's shoe, and so Billy had permanent scuffs on all of his pairs of shoes from frequent use of his guider. Today, this form of activity would be condemned as far too dangerous for kids, without helmets and padding. What a pity! It was such awesome fun!

The rest of the time, most of the local kids played hours of football. They used to congregate in the summer holidays, in Abbots Cross school yard, which had a sloping field. Every kid in the street could climb the school fence easily, to gain access, although technically they were all trespassing on council land. Teams were picked and could be up to about 15 a side, or as little as two people per side. As long as there was someone left to kick a ball, football was continuous and they just kept picking teams from who was available. Often, Billy would go in for his tea, after a game and come back out, half an hour later ready to join another game. It made them all decent players in the end and some of his friends even forged football careers out of all that incessant practice!

Billy was always a good organiser and so once or twice during the school holidays, he would recruit the local kids to play 'Olympics' in the school yard. It involved various races, throwing pram wheels and metal poles and even archery using home-made bows. No one ever got hurt, as Billy always planned it with safety in mind and it was a great change from the usual everyday football marathons. The medals were all made of cardboard, but the kids themselves had the prestige of being seen, as the best runner, jumper or thrower in the street. Billy himself got sick of always losing the sprint races to Geordie and Paul and finally realised that if he did a race of 20 or more laps around the block, where he lived, he could beat their asses at last! This endurance ability came into the fore much later, when as an adult he completed several Belfast and Dublin City Marathons.

Back at school, Billy got a small part, singing in a version of the Dickens classic 'Oliver', when he was eight and he really enjoyed it. By the time he was ten, everyone had realised he was quite a good boy soprano. The music teacher, Mr. Murray used to visit each class in the school on one or two afternoons a week. He did Singing lessons with every class and he taught the kids how to properly play rhythms and use percussion instruments. The BBC did music workshops for schools on the radio in those days and

Mr. Murray was well organised. He paid for all the singing books and accessories, that went with these workshops and the music lessons were great fun. He also took after school choir, two days per week and Billy loved it. They all had to learn several songs in the Gaelic language at one point and Billy was reluctant to partake, as this was culturally conflicting with his desire to be accepted as a loyalist protestant. Ironically, He was the best male soloist in the school and so Mr. Murray persuaded him to compete in a Belfast Feis at The 'Ard Scoil' on the Lower Falls Road. (A 'Feis' is the Irish name for a festival of Gaelic Arts). To his embarrassment, he stormed it and came first. By the end of the night, Billy was the owner of a beautiful winners' medal. He was chuffed to have won, but sadly he couldn't boast about his win to his Protestant family or friends, as they would never appreciate any association with Irish traditional arts. In that respect he felt like an accidental traitor to the Loyalist cause.

In spite of everything, Billy did very well at Stella Maris Primary School and after a cracking 11plus exam pass, he was accepted into St. Malachys College, a prestigious Catholic Grammar school. At first this was a great adventure and so different from his relatively cosy little primary school. He had heard about the school's academic reputation and that even some protestant employers apparently gave jobs to ex-students from that school. His positive outlook changed as soon as the Nationalist 'Provo' fanatics who also attended St. Malachy's, became politically active, while the Northern Ireland 'Troubles' steadily escalated. Once again Billy was the victim of a barrage of verbal and physical abuse. Almost daily, he was punched, often kicked in the groin, and called a Proddy lover and a snout! The worst part was the abusers who created large green 'hockles' in their mouths, then spat on his hair and on the back of his school blazer, as he walked past. His school blazer had to be washed in his mum's Burco boiler, due to the amount of disgusting spit that had accumulated on the back. Consequently, Jeanette was always buying new blazers, as after a few washes they lost their shape and looked tatty. Billy was even asked on more than one occasion 'Are you a Provo or a Stickie? He had to ask someone what a Stickie was. It turned out that anyone who supported the old original IRA, was classed as a 'Stickie' and the modern active Republicans were the 'Provisionals' or 'Provos. He even lied and said he was a 'Stickie' once, as he thought it sounded better than saying, 'Oh, I am actually a loyalist and I would dearly love to shoot all you bloody bullyboy Fenians!'

St. Malachy's was in the middle of Belfast, about 5 miles away from his home and so Billy had to travel on the number 161a, Rathcoole to Belfast bus every day. His school badge clearly showed that he was a Catholic and so the journey to and from home often became a game of running the gauntlet. He was frequently picked on by Rathcoole kids on the bus and in the street. As a result of one of these beatings, Jeanette complained to the school and Billy was given special permission to wear a plain grey jumper without the famous green and black stripes of St. Malachys, on the collar trim. He also put his school badge onto press studs, that could be pulled off his blazer quickly. This meant that when he took off his school tie, no one could tell what school he attended. Eventually the beatings stopped, even though the empty studs on his empty blazer pocket, made people ask curious questions about what he had to hide.

St. Malachy's College was run by priests and they had a strong code of discipline. They had two Deans, who basically enforced the regime and they caned students on the hands, if they so much as walked down the corridor on the wrong side. They seemed to enjoy physically hurting the students and sent fear into the hearts of anyone who was nearby. One of the Deans was nicknamed 'Smiley' because of his sadistic grinning, as he caned each child. The cane was bamboo, about three feet long, rounded like a drumstick and nearly two centimetres thick. They made students bend their fingers right back, when getting caned, so you could nearly see the bones through the skin and then they skilfully hit the inside of the top knuckles, so that the fingers stayed bruised for days. If anyone tried to pull their hand away, they ended up getting two more smacks on each hand with the cane. The other Dean was called Father Murtagh and he was very tall and lanky, with a particular long neck. He walked with a noticeably springy, bounce in his step and became known to students as 'Rubberman' or 'The Bounce'. It perfectly described his unique style of walking. He also had a third nickname 'Brrdoingg', which just mimicked the sound of a recoiling spring. He was just as sadistic as Smiley, although his trademark was sarcasm, rather than an evil smile. Between them it was, tantamount to blatant child abuse and it wasn't only the sadistic Deans who behaved in this way. Many of the other teachers delighted in punching students or twisting their ears for example, if they got questions wrong in lessons. The old Monty Python sketch from 'The Life of Brian', about Brian getting the Latin word endings wrong and getting his ear twisted by the Centurion, is exactly how things were done in Billy's school. He genuinely forgot to do a Mathematics homework on one occasion and at just 12 years old was properly and sadistically 'gut' punched, by a powerfully built Mathematics teacher, who was definitely not a priest. He lay on the classroom floor crying in pain, under the desk for a full 5 minutes, until 'Smiley' came along and removed him from the lesson. Smiley decided to give Billy a detention for not doing the homework, however, he didn't bat an eyelid about the teacher's sadistic act of punching a young student! Billy told his Dad about these beatings, but it turned out his Dad had taken far worse in his school days and he simply told him to stop whingeing, be a man and that he must have deserved it. These were collectively warped and scary religious fanatics, who took pride in upholding their disciplinary regime, not unlike the Nazis during the second World War. These were the unfortunate delights of a strict 1970s Catholic education, in Belfast! The system was meant to make you a tougher man for the outside world! No wonder so many ex-students ended up as evil IRA terrorists! By the time the law changed years later, to protect children from these sadistic fascists, it was far too late for Billy's generation and so the mental scars were there for life. Imagine getting PTSD from just attending school. How Dickensian is that?

St. Malachy's taught only GAA sports and it was always Gaelic football, basketball, hurling and Handball every day, instead of Soccer, tennis and cricket. Billy could never dribble the ball up into his hands, the way the Gaelic players did, but he was a fast, natural and gifted winger with a powerful left foot, at soccer (real football). He could not believe that in Gaelic football, you were permitted to punch the ball into the goal with the front of your fist. That was a blatant 'Handball' and a penalty kick in real football? The unshakeable coach used to blow his whistle and at least once a week, he was heard to shout 'McCree, you are playing soccer again, that's not how we dribble in Gaelic football!... Detention, after school!' Billy would shout back 'Sorry Sir, but I can only play soccer!' Often that would be followed up by the coach with 'It's time you bloody learned!'

The school also had a training ground about two miles from the main school and they used an old London bus, which was hand-painted in the school colours to ferry the students back and forward. The ground was called Marmont and it had three large Gaelic football pitches and a running track on a very hilly area at the top of the Cliftonville Road in Belfast. It was so open and so high up above Belfast, that it was always bloody freezing up there, even in good weather. One day in a PE lesson, Billy and four other classmates hid in a little enclave on top of some bins, to get out of a horrific blizzard. They should have been taking part in a Gaelic match out on the pitch. It was perishing and you couldn't even see the ball on the pitch, with the heavy snow and freezing winds. They were caught red handed, by the irate, grumpy coach, as they perched on top of the large bins.

All five students were given a standard one hour, after school detention. Back in school, they explained to the Detention Duty teacher that they had been trying to escape the icy blizzard. He was horrified, as he had been watching the insane weather from his classroom window earlier and thought that it would not be very nice at all to be caught in it, let alone try to play sport. He agreed that the coach had been over-zealous to punish them. This thankfully, sensible teacher, signed them off and let them all go home.

Billy had two friends in his class at school, who lived in the nearby Protestant Monkstown estate. They were very much like him and would have preferred to have been brought up as protestants too. They used to chat together at the bus stop in the afternoons, after school, usually about football and music. On one occasion a notorious Rathcoole Protestant extremist 'Scar' Robinson was at the end of the same bus stop queue. They knew of him and asked if Billy did too. All three were terrified of this guy's reputation for beating up Catholics and they all had heard the rumour that he was supposed to have stabbed someone on a least one occasion. There was a little bit of eyeballing going on, but they didn't dare speak to Scar. Years later this seemingly innocuous encounter, came back to haunt Billy while having a quiet drink in the Merville Inn. Scar and an accomplice walked up to Billy and accused him, in front of friends of 'singling' him out to known Nationalists, all those years before. This was just a bollocks excuse made up to create a reason for a fight. Billy claimed he was going to the toilet and would sort this matter out with him, when he came back to finish his drink. Instead, he ran out the door as soon as he was out of sight of the dreaded Scar. In his anxiety and fear and a massive buzz from his adrenal glands, Billy tripped over the high step at the front door of the pub and twisted his left ankle badly. He ignored this pain and ran for nearly a mile, never looking behind him. Scar never caught up with him though! It was strange how the adrenalin rush from the serious threat of danger, allowed Billy to run at full pelt for such a distance, with his injured ankle, yet once he stopped running and felt safe, he realised he could not actually walk or put his weight on the injured foot. It took him quite a while, but in the end, he limped home safely. He thankfully, never encountered the dreaded 'Scar' again.

Chapter 3:

Beliefs and Loyalties

Ironically, and thanks to the influence of his dad, Billy McCree really was a proper Orangeman in the making. Alan always felt hurt that he couldn't bring his kids up the way he wanted. His own family made him sick of religion with all their hypocrisy and arguments about different 'interpretations' of the bible and so only his love for Jeanette and acceptance of her fears of going against the Catholic church stopped him from complaining. In those days you could still be excommunicated for disobeying the rules of the Catholic church. Jeanette was British at heart though, as her proud father had served King George V in India and in WW1. All five of her brothers then followed their father and served in the various branches of the British military.

Jeanette just let Alan get on with all the Orange Loyalist stuff, as she regarded the whole family as British Unionists anyway and really wasn't bothered about any of it. Alan did make sure that he took Billy and his siblings to the Shankill Road and Sandy Row bonfires every 11th July and the whole family including Jeanette, attended the Belfast Orange parades every 12th of July, without fail. Billy 'kicked the Pope', with all the other Orangemen. Greasy Chips and Coca Cola were the 'norm' for him and his siblings, as they invariably sat on the kerb on the Dublin Road, outside the Elbow Room Pub, just in front of the BBC camera stand, waving hand-held union flags and enjoying the many lodges and bands proudly marching past in the massive 'Twelfth' celebrations. They learned to sing the Sash, No Surrender,

The Green Grassy slopes of the Boyne and many other Protestant hymns, as they waved their union flags at the annual celebrations.

Billy used to love the build up to the 'Twelfth' also, as for weeks before it, the kids in his street gathered wood, old car tyres, used mattresses, broken chairs etc and competed to build the biggest bonfire on the estate. They used to take saws and axes up Carnmoney Hill (the local woods and beauty spot) and come back dragging huge tree branches for the bonfire. On one occasion, they ran into a gang from Glenbane Avenue, who always famously, had the biggest bonfire on the estate. Billy and his friends had taken packed lunches with them and these kids were trying to bully them into handing over their lunch. He detested all bullies, because of his school experiences and was determined to keep a hold of his sandwiches and coffee, so he turned and ran like hell. Assuming they were still chasing him, he tried to slide down a very steep part of the hill. He slipped and literally did four complete somersaults, before coming to a halt at the bottom. It was a bit like that scene with Jack Sparrow inside the windmill wheel in Pirates of the Caribbean II. He could have very easily broken his neck, but luckily, the only casualty was his coffee flask, which smashed in his backpack. At least he got away from the bullies, with only a few bruises for his trouble. Of course, neither he nor his friends managed to collect any wood that day.

Later that evening, by way of trying to make up for their lost efforts, his friend Stan climbed a tree, which was behind the garages in their street. It was also very close to where their bonfire was going to be built. It was always thought that this tree could not be cut down for 'Boney' (bonfire) wood, due to its' close-proximity to the houses in their street. A focussed and determined Stan had a huge bow saw in his hand and decided he was going to climb up and cut down a certain large branch, to add to the bonfire wood. He was feeling extremely pleased with himself, when after a short period of intense sawing, the targeted branch fell away towards the ground. He then watched in terror as it caught a telephone wire on the way down and ripped it from the nearby telegraph pole. The connection at the other end sheared away from the wall of a nearby house and the seething occupants immediately called the police. They also claimed that their phone had shot up the wall, inside the house. Stan's dad had to pay for the telephone engineer to do substantial repairs and he himself, now had an official Police reprimand for criminal damage.

In the days before the 11th of July, it was necessary for some of the street kids to camp out beside the fire, as gangs of kids from other rival bonfires tended to try to steal wood, for their own fires. Billy took his turn camping out on a number of occasions, as they often had to chase other kids off in the wee small hours, to stop them stealing their 'Boney' wood! This was usually uneventful, but there had been a few serious fights over the years, between rival gangs, in the middle of the night, when 'Boney' wood went missing. Billy punched a kid from another gang one night, who had bullied his friend Stan, but he then had to sneak back home and leave his tent, after the kid returned with his big brother and five other lads, looking to sort Billy out! It was just how things were.

There were other ways in which you knew the local kids were building up for the Twelfth celebrations, like when they used to make their own Mace poles with painted brush shafts and decorated them with home-made baubles and strips of coloured wool stuck onto them. They then paraded down the middle of the road, leading their fictitious Orange bands. Some of the kids in the street were like American baton twirlers and could skilfully spin and throw their poles up to twenty feet or so, in the air and catch them, just like the real live flute band leaders. Other kids beat the shit out of old biscuit tins, tied around their necks with cord, pretending they were playing marching snare drums. One powerfully built kid on one occasion, unbelievably carried an old metal council rubbish bin, tied on to his waist and neck with ropes, as a fairly effective and very noisy bass drum. The best bit was the few kids in the street who had tin whistles and kazoos and actually could play the traditional Orange tunes on them. It was great fun, but the horrendous racket from the badly co-ordinated collective of pseudo-musicians, must have driven the older residents in the neighbourhood mental.

Many years later, when Billy was a working man, the 12th of July got to be very heated and controversial. The differences between the political factions deepened, as the Troubles progressed. It meant that sometimes the 12th of July was just an excuse for both sides to exacerbate the tensions in Northern Ireland's religious conflict. On other occasions, it could still be enjoyed, as an annual celebration of Protestantism and the 1690 victory over the Jacobite army at the Boyne river.

The parade used to pass too close to some Nationalist areas and these became hot spots for riots, with both sides inciting each other. It often depended on things like the weather that week, or what political events including shootings, had been happening in the build up to the Twelfth, as to whether it was going to be a fun time or just a brutal mini civil war.

Billy and his brother, Joseph, had never been allowed to join the Orange order, because of their Mother being a Catholic and because they had attended Catholic schools themselves. There were strict rules in the Lodges. This meant that they would often choose to wander along to the start of the Belfast Twelfth Parade near Carlisle Circus, with a crate of beer, bought the night before. Then they just walked alongside the parade, drinking as they went to the field at beautiful Lagan Valley and back into Belfast centre in the late afternoon. They would often find a band they liked or a local lodge with marchers that they knew and just tag along, guzzling the beer, as they went. They took turns carrying their heavy booze and found that the best way to carry it, was to drink it quickly. They also had fun visiting just about every public loo and Bar toilet along the route.

One year, the pre-twelfth atmosphere between the Orangemen and the Nationalists was so bad that it lead to mass riots in quite a few rural areas, as well as in Londonderry and Belfast. Billy and Joseph sensed the pre-twelfth mood was a bit more dangerous than usual and decided just to get out of town for a few days, instead of attending the marches. They hitch-hiked to Dublin, of all places. They went off with a tent, backpacks and a guitar on the morning of the 11th of July and got to the old Butlin's Mosney camp, by mid-afternoon. Billy was chuffed because it felt like a pilgrimage to be beside the famous river Boyne at the Twelfth. He even took a walk by the river to more clearly imagine the Battle back in July 1690. That evening, they had managed to put up their tent, had dinner in the camp restaurant and were relaxing in the large ballroom. After only a few minutes, Billy made straight for a extremely attractive young redhead that he had spotted, a short distance away and asked her to dance. She was called Roisin and was there with her sister and her two small kids, for the weekend. Joseph wasn't very eloquent with the fair sex and he hated dancing, so he just sat and enjoyed his beer and let his older brother indulge his insanely rampant hormones. Billy was giving it everything on the dance floor and wasting their limited resources buying drink for his new lady friend and her sister. By the end of the night, he and his floozy were ready to hump the night away. Roisin, like a good catholic girl, told him she was married, but didn't mind a bit of extramarital fun and suggested they use Billy's tent, while her sister tucked the kids up in their caravan. Just then, the heavens opened and by midnight the rain was torrential. The entertainment buildings were now locked and so a desperately horny Billy, had to say no to this attractive lady, as it would mean leaving his brother walking around in a monsoon, while he did his bit to improve North/South relations in the tent. Joseph said he would not have minded, but what kind of selfish brother would that have made Billy?

He was feeling bad about the wasted opportunity for a rampant sexual encounter with a married nymphomaniac, but at least he had arranged to meet the lovely Roisin again in Dublin City centre, the next day.

Early the next morning, they rolled up the soaking wet tent and headed into Dublin. After a short time thumbing a lift, a friendly local farmer, picked them up and dropped them right in the middle of O'Connell Street. Joseph was keen to see and photograph the famous bullet holes in the Post Office walls from the 1916 Easter Rising and they both loved the old Georgian architecture and the historic feel of the City centre. Money was running low and so Billy headed up to Grafton Street for 3 hours of busking. He later met up with his lady friend Roisin, as agreed. Joseph discreetly went for a walk and kindly took his brother's guitar with him along with the tent and backpack. Billy had a lovely hour and a half with Roisin in a pub, drinking and snogging and talking crap. Roisin tasted and smelt lovely too. They talked a lot and then exchanged phone numbers. Billy was still keen and promised to come back down to visit her from Belfast, as soon as he could. He was definitely liking this girl! Roisin suddenly started to look edgy and then hurriedly left. It seems she was meeting her husband straight after him. 'The brazen bitch, he thought!' Billy met back up with Joseph at the other end of O'Connell Street and they headed towards the bus stop for Dublin airport, where they had planned to spend the night, in the arrivals lounge. They both didn't fancy another night in a sopping wet tent. Suddenly Joseph spotted Roisin across the road, walking hand in hand with her husband and looking like butter wouldn't melt. 'She is trouble that one Bruv, I wouldn't waste any more time on her, if I were you!' Joseph said. Billy looked thoughtful and reluctantly agreed, shaking his head disconsolately, as they jumped on the bus to Dublin airport. The next morning, after an uncomfortable, cramped night, lying under plastic chairs in sleeping bags in the Arrivals lounge, they bought croissants and coffee at one of the airport outlets and then headed back into Dublin to finish their sightseeing. By mid-afternoon, the brothers decided to start the journey back to Belfast. North of Dublin an accountant picked them up on the Belfast Road, but he was only going as far as Dundalk. They walked carefully through the town of Dundalk, after he dropped them, as it was a notorious hang out for Provo fugitives hiding from the British Army in the North. They started to thumb a lift again and very soon, a friendly greyhound owner invited them to get into the back of his van beside his two prize dogs. Billy wasn't sure, as he was allergic to dogs and he also had asthma, but he had to make the most of the opportunity of a lift. Both dogs were muzzled, which helped. He still sneezed constantly, with both eyes swollen and he struggled to breath for the whole journey. The dogs were trying to snuggle up to them in the confined space too. The driver dropped Billy and Joseph about three miles from the border and so they started walking on the road again, as darkness began to fall. 'Thank God that's over Joseph, I couldn't have taken the air in that car, anymore!' Billy gasped. He was tired by now, but put his backpack on and lifted the guitar, which he carried in his arms in front of him. After a full half hour of walking and the worrying thought of having to walk for half the night, a car finally stopped. A voice shouted out of the open car window 'What the hell are you two playing at? Don't you know this is bandit territory?' Billy and Joseph anxiously looked into the car. The voice then said 'The Provos have secret camps around here to hide out from the Brits!' You look just like a bloody soldier carrying his rifle, in the dark.' Joseph glanced at Billy. 'Shit, he is right! In the shadows, the way you are carrying your guitar, you could be a soldier, Billy!'. The owner of the voice, laughed mockingly and said 'Get in, are you heading North? I am going as far as Newry!' It turned out he was a Newry farmer and dropped them at a garage, just back inside Northern Ireland. Billy breathed a sigh of relief, that at least they no longer stuck on that awful dark road from Dundalk.

It was now just before 11pm and the garage was about to shut for the night. One lonely Ford Fiesta pulled in to fill up with petrol. Billy told Joseph to hang fire for a moment. He looked thoughtful, then instinctively ran across to the parked car and immediately pleaded with the driver to take them to Belfast. He knew that they would have had to camp in a field otherwise. He even joked that he would sing them a song right there and then, in the garage forecourt, if the driver agreed to take them further north. The slightly bemused driver and his male companion were in fact heading for Larne to get the late-night ferry to Stranraer, in Scotland. They weren't entirely sure of the route and so Billy keenly said he could show them the correct roads to take and even show them a short cut, if they had a map. This meant that they could drop Billy and Joseph within a mile and a half of home, in Rathcoole, with only a minimum of disruption to their journey. The driver agreed to take them and without further ado the brothers jumped into the back seats of the little car. When they disembarked they had to walk on the actual road surface of the M2 motorway for about 400metres, to get back to the Shore Road, but it was after 1am and the roads were empty. They eventually arrived back home in Rathcoole exhausted from their adventures, at around 2am.

During their trip away, Billy had been talking to Joseph in great depth about their unique childhood experiences growing up in a mixed marriage. He told his brother in great detail, about the time he spent in his two senior years at St. Malachys. It was one of the few times in his life that he hadn't been bullied. In his step up to senior school, the class sets had been reorganised. Luckily, the lads in his class were more normal and not the Nationalist bullies that he had been used to. He relaxed more and got on with trying to catch up on his education for his GCE O levels. It was difficult, as the traumatic bullying of the first 3 years at St. Malachy's, had left him trailing academically behind other students.

At the age of 15, Billy had also joined the local Presbyterian Boys Brigade at Rathcoole's Belfast City Mission. This was mainly to get playing football with the BB team. Bizarrely, on Sundays after morning Mass at Whitehouse Catholic Church, he headed straight up to the BB bible class. Attendance at the bible class was obligatory and meant that he automatically qualified to play football for the BB team, the following Saturday. This had been a challenge at first, as the senior players were all in the local tartan gang, called the

'KAI', which stood for 'Kill all Irishmen'. This group was in effect the under 18s version of the UVF. They suspiciously viewed Billy as a Fenian and some of them wouldn't even pass the ball to him during league games, because of their unfounded bias. Billy was quite a decent footballer, but their attitude totally isolated him and undermined his self-confidence. When he did play, he often found it hard to concentrate and made loads of mistakes, because of his constant awareness of their contemptuous monitoring of his play and their blatant name calling, laughing and discrimination. The team manager was the BB Captain's son and so the team was his 'baby' and he did what he liked, choosing only who he wanted to play. He knew about the bullying and didn't choose Billy very often for the team, as he knew his favourites wouldn't like it! So most often, Billy was one of the substitutes and if he did get to play, it was usually only 10 or 15 minutes, at the end of a game. He spent many cold Saturday afternoons just sitting on the team minibus, waiting for someone to ask him to come and play!

After about a year, these older players left the Boys Brigade, because they had turned 18 and some of them had work and other adult things to do. Suddenly Billy was getting picked every week and he was playing out of his skin, with two or three really Class players alongside him, making the 16th Newtownabbey, one of the top and feared Boys Brigade teams. They had one player, Raymond McAlister, who was like a cross between George Best and Paul Gascoigne. Raymond used to get annoyed with the rest of the team, as he couldn't understand why they couldn't do what he did with the ball, like beat 7 of the opposition at a time, before scoring amazing goals. The Manager couldn't believe the difference in Billy's game that season. He just felt better at the trust now being put in him and his confidence grew along with his ability.

As he reached his older teenage years, the bullying eventually stopped and Billy became just one of the boys. His mates gradually forgave him for attending a Fenian school and some of them even understood the complicated religious blackmail that had tied his fathers' hands all those years ago. Full acceptance as an honorary Protestant came, when he became the company band leader and led the 16th Newtownabbey to the annual Belfast Battalion BB parade and awards at the Belfast Presbyterian Assembly buildings and then proudly into the island town of Millport in Scotland in June 1974, for BB summer camp. Billy attained all his level 2 badges that year and was subsequently promoted to lance corporal and given his own squad. The local Pastor and the BB Captain knew his mixed religious background, but as true Christians they supported Billy and they quietly viewed him attending the Protestant church as a victory over the misguided Catholics.

Chapter 4:

The Beautiful Game

In Northern Ireland, the football was always only at semi-professional standard. This meant that for instance, Linfield's goalkeeper may have been an insurance man by day, Glentoran's top goal scorer was perhaps a shipyard fitter or Crusaders Captain, a part-time television journalist. This situation meant that many fans seeking to support a top professional team, either followed the obvious religious divisions and supported Celtic or Rangers in Scotland, or they went for Manchester United in England, as an apparent eternal, but somewhat baffling sympathetic consequence of the 1958 Munich air disaster.

The next-door neighbour, Tommy Johnston was a big Linfield fan. His son Geordie was a close friend of Billy's and so this led to his first experience of a real football match at 9 years old. Tommy took them both to see Linfield play Ards at Windsor Park, in the old Gold Cup competition. Billy's own dad Alan, had no interest in football and so Tommy introduced Billy to the atmosphere, crowd, excitement and sheer overwhelming fun of the greatest sport in the world. Linfield won 2-1 and he went to a few more games after that. Tommy used to get Geordie and Billy to wash up the beer glasses in the Rathcoole Branch of the Linfield Supporters Club, on a Sunday morning, after a busy Saturday of entertainment. They were well paid for their trouble and got free snacks and coke too.

Tommy was the Secretary for that branch and Billy was in awe of how much passion and love he had for his football club. In the long term, Billy became a fan of Crusaders, as their ground Seaview, was much closer to home and unlike Linfield, they didn't have exclusively Protestant supporters. They also had a cracking team and threatened 'The Blues' dominance. Linfield were the Belfast equivalent of Rangers in Scotland and so Catholics were not welcome.

Billy was told around that time, that he should follow Manchester United, by just about every kid in school. He did like Celtic. Who wouldn't? Jock Stein's 1967 European Champions were sublime. As his love for the beautiful game developed, Billy realised he really liked that big Liverpool centre-half Ron Yeats and a certain goal scorer called Roger Hunt, along with his 'larger than life' strike partner, Ian St. John. He watched an embryonic ' Match of the Day' on telly one night, when Best, Law and Charlton tore Liverpool apart at Anfield and won 4-1. Billy got angry at the arrogance of the Mancunians and felt sorry for the Reds. Even in those times, he couldn't understand the apparent media bias towards the Manchester club. Once Billy realised that in Northern Ireland only Catholics supported Celtic, he began to cement a beautiful and lifelong relationship with the Scousers. In 1971 Arsenal's double winning team stole the FA Cup from Liverpool after Steve Heighway had given the Reds the lead, thanks to a late Charlie George goal. An inconsolable 13year-old, spent the night in his room bawling his eyes out. From that day on Liverpool became the love of his life!

Football was a great way of getting away from the troubles. Rathcoole had heroes like Jimmy Nicholl (Manchester United), Jimmy Quinn (Swindon and West Ham) and Johnny Jamison (Huddersfield Town). They set the standard for all those Boys Brigade players like Billy. His friend Raymond once played in a BB Battalion game against Liverpool Battalion and was immediately offered trials with Tottenham and Man United. Linfield were the biggest club in Northern Ireland and asked him just to turn up and train the following week with their third team, with the chance of signing terms with them, straight away. Unfortunately, Raymond had discovered women and booze around the same time and so nothing ever came of his footballing potential. Billy was in complete despair, as he would have loved to have had this opportunity, but he never made the Battalion team. Much to Billy's dismay, Raymond wasted his football talent and instead became a beer-bellied fitter in the Belfast shipyard.

After leaving school at 16 with just 5 O levels, a disillusioned Billy joined the civil service. To him education was only about the rich kids getting opportunities and he always felt the school treated him as a potential low achiever, partly because of his mixed religious background and partly because school represented daily bullying and fear. He used his meagre qualifications to get a job as a Tax clerk for the Inland Revenue and even became an influential Trade Unionist for a short time, rising to Branch Secretary for Northern Ireland Revenue staff. Suddenly he had enough money to go to Liverpool matches and consequently spent quite a few weekends attending their home games.

This dedication went on for the next 15 years. He formed a bond with a lad called Davy Simpson in his street and they even managed to start a branch of the Liverpool supporters club, in his friend's family home of Lisburn. The full title was 'Ist Lisnagarvey Liverpool Supporters Club'. They used to torture friends, family and workmates, constantly selling poker tickets to finance trips to their beloved Anfield. On one occasion 19 of them were about to get The Ulster Prince ferry boat back to Belfast, after a Liverpool home game. The secretary said it was the end of the financial year and they would have to pay tax as a supporters club, if they didn't spend their excess funds. With two hours until the boat left, they all went to the pub at Pier Head and ordered 95 pints of lager, five pints each, to use up some of the money. The club also paid for their dinner on board ship. What a trip home that was!

Billy loved to tell the stories to the other club members, such as how he went by Larne/Stranraer and then the train, to Wolverhampton in May 1976, to see Liverpool clinch the league title. The English pubs closed at 3pm in those days and so he was drunk in the middle of Wolverhampton, singing Liverpool songs four hours before the game. A group of Scouse lads, spotted him and warned him he could get a kicking wandering around Wolverhampton on his own, wearing his red scarf. They turned out to be squaddies on leave from Northern Ireland, to see the game. They had a car, with a boot full of sandwiches, coffee and beer and they thought Billy was the craziest, loudest and most amusing fan they had ever met. He had a ready-made bunch of mates for the night. Billy recklessly hadn't booked a return trip or a hotel and so they looked after their new friend. Bizarrely, he ended up on a crammed M6, sitting with the others on the roof of their car at 2am and singing Scouse anthems till their throats ached. The M6 was a road party of delirious Liverpool fans that night and even the Champions team bus got stuck in the party traffic that night. He eventually got into Liverpool at 4am and was dropped at Pier Head, where a friendly taxi driver managed to get him into a hotel somewhere in the suburbs, for what was left of this very happy night. He asked the Night Porter not to waken him before 12 noon. Billy spent the whole of the next day wandering around Liverpool on a happy cloud, until it was time to catch the evening ferry back to Belfast.

The following season, Liverpool drew Crusaders in the European Cup (now the Champions League). Billy wore his Liverpool scarf to the match at Seaview, to the dismay of his friends and argued 'Crusaders are my local team, but Liverpool are the love of my life, my passion and joy!' They won 7-0 on aggregate against the semi-pros from Belfast. It has to be said, Crusaders had only lost 2-0 at Anfield in the first leg and were much better defensively than some of the top English sides that season.

His other favourite story took place on 16 March 1977. Billy took an afternoon flight to Liverpool from Belfast. He had no ticket for the famous St. Etienne game in the European cup quarter final. An hour before kick-off, he was queueing hopefully in Kemlyn Road, beside the Kop. It was touch and go whether he would get in, as they didn't have strict all ticket rules in those days and the crowd was expected to be huge. Luckily, a friendly police horse decided to pee for England at one point and as about 1000 or so fans moved hurriedly away from the resultant tidal wave, Billy leapt across a huge pool of horse piss and accidentally jumped the queue. He did get some of the horse's deluge on his shoes and in his socks, but 'hey, anything to see the Reds!'

Shortly after, Billy completed the pilgrimage into his beloved Kop. He was only in the door and with just two other people getting in behind him, he heard the stewards getting the order to close the gates. Ten thousand fans didn't get in that night. Thank you so much for your lack of bladder control, police horse! Once on the Kop, the famous swaying and singing started. The Kop had never been so packed. It was painful holding people back and Billy was ready for a very uncomfortable time. Suddenly two very large twins in red bomber jackets and scarves pushed in front of him. They were built like huge wrestlers and when the crowd moved forward, amazingly Billy could manoeuvre himself in front and slightly between them and they held dozens of fans back from the barrier. No matter how much cheering and moving went on in the crowd, Billy was now covered and protected by his powerful neighbours. He didn't get squashed even once after that. The game was amazing and thanks to David Fairclough's late goal, their dream of conquering Europe continued. He met some other fans from Belfast in the Park Bar, behind the Kop, after the match and after two hours of riding around in a taxi and not being able to find suitable accommodation, they all slept on the floor of the arrivals lounge at Speke Airport, with their overcoats as blankets.

They all flew back to Belfast together the next morning.

In 1978, Billy was working briefly in London with the Inland Revenue. His contract finished a few days before the European Cup final, but he wouldn't go home. He waited until the afternoon of 10th May, then proceeded to Wembley where he paid £50 for a £12 ticket. Ticket touting was still accepted then and he didn't care how much it cost, so long as he got to see Liverpool. He met dozens of his old friends from Northern Ireland, as they had travelled with coach trips and only paid face value for their ticket. Liverpool beat FC Bruges 1-0, thanks to his hero Kenny Dalglish's goal and so Billy flew back to Belfast the next day, buzzing with pride and sheer joy.

In 1982, Billy went with the Supporters club to the famous Everton 0-5 Liverpool and saw the legendary Ian Rush score 4 goals. They got off the ferry from Belfast at 6:30am and went in taxis to a little pub called the Tugboat in Netherfield Road. With a secret knock you could get in from 5am. It was crammed full of nightshift workers, who had called in for an early morning pint before going home. It was only about 7am, but Billy never saw anything like it! That morning they only stayed till 9am, as they needed tickets for the game. It was all ticket, but only about 8 of their party had tickets, so Billy and his friend Davy walked around the perimeter of Goodison Park, as they had done outside Anfield many times. Within a half hour they had bought a ticket for double the face value. Once again remembering that back then, no one cared about touting genuine tickets and counterfeiting tickets wasn't a problem like today.

At another game, the boys went to, what he was told was a Protestant Loyalist bar in Liverpool. They went there straight off the ferry at 7am and were told to drink up by 10am. Billy thought this strange, since they were already drinking out of hours, but the staff explained that they were actually attending an Orange march in Southport later that day and the lodge was at that moment assembling outside the club. 'My God' Billy thought, 'They have Orange lodges in Liverpool too!' He was chuffed and a little bit bemused, as he naively didn't realise Orangeism was such a big deal in Liverpool, until then. The lodge proceeded to march to Lime Street station, complete with their own accordian band, where they were met by family members with their luggage and off they all went to Southport for a day of marching.

Every Liverpool trip was an adventure and there was always a story to tell by the end of it. Just before Christmas one year, Billy's mate Davy decided to take his little Renault on the Larne/Stranraer ferry. They brought his friend Adam from work along with them and his teenage son Gerry, who was a Spurs fan. Liverpool were of course, playing Spurs in a league match and they drove down overnight from Scotland. They tried to sleep in the car but around 4am, in a car park just outside Morecambe, the local Police decided they were having none of it and moved them on. No sleep for anyone that night then! The next day Liverpool won the match 2-1, but Adam had to rescue Gerry from a group of aggressive Liverpool fans who wanted to kick his head in, just for wearing a Spurs scarf. Adam was wearing his Liverpool scarf and explained that it was normal for someone's kid to support a different team. Billy was only told about it after the game, as he had gone into the Kop alone. He was angry at his own fellow Liverpool supporters, as The Reds were generally very sporting, but like every club in the 70s and 80s there were some nutters, who just used their football rivalry as an excuse for a fight. Afterwards they drove to Southport and stayed in a small Hotel, where Adam claimed he had stayed on his honeymoon, 16 years earlier. He was getting very sentimental about being there and chattering on about his wife. Billy didn't understand this, as he had never been in love up to that point. The trip home in the car was as uncomfortable as before, with little leg room for his skinny 6 foot frame, all the way to Cairnryan on the Galloway coast. To add to that, the rough seas of the North Channel made Billy seasick for the whole two and a half-hour sea crossing and he spent most of the journey in the same cubicle in the Gents toilet. He still felt it was all worth it to see the Reds win and he wore his discomfort as a badge of loyalty to his club!

Chapter 5:

The Rocker

Billy loved all the rock music that was around in the 1970s. Starting with a love for glam rock kings Slade at 12 years old. He even made his own Noddy Holder hat with corn flake boxes and Sellotape and then decorated it with black Fablon and silver circles of kitchen foil. As he grew and explored music further, he realised there were some great guitar bands around. His friends loaned him albums by Deep Purple, Thin Lizzy and the band who became his ultimate favourites, Status Quo. They all registered with Billy's sense of what really rocked!

He had always felt inclined to learn to play guitar, since he was little and used to sing along with his mum's Beatles records. When he was 5 years old, he used to play air guitar to Shadows records too. He even took part in an 'air guitar' band in school, when he was just 6. Four of them would go round the other classes in school singing 'She loves you' and 'Can't buy me love' while strumming invisible guitars at the same time. Alan could never afford to buy him an instrument, as guitars were not cheap. Unfortunately, Billy's grammar school only taught students how to play classical instruments, as they regarded pop music as a joke. Also due to an asthma condition, he could never manage to breathe correctly to learn to play a wind instrument. It took until he was 16 and working, with only his second monthly Civil Service wage, before he bought a basic second-hand folk guitar. Billy tried for weeks with the help of a Bert Weedon guitar tutorial book, but he couldn't get his chords to sound right. The problem was he could never keep the guitar in tune properly. The pitch pipes that he bought, had a totally different timbre from the guitar, which made it difficult for an untrained ear. In the end he paid privately for just 6 guitar lessons. These few lessons were enough to learn tuning techniques and basic chords and then he slowly taught himself the rest at home, mostly playing along with his rock records after that.

In time he bought a sleek, black Antoria Les Paul together with an HH VS Musician 100watt amplifier. The amp had a full array of bright green lights on all the controls and looked fantastic. That was why he bought it. It really did look the part, but in a gig situation, it didn't always project the sound out far enough and often punters complained they couldn't hear his lead solos! It was all about image though! Within a year and after many hours of practice in his room, Billy began his next lifelong love of playing in rock bands. He used to drive the family mad for 2 to 3 hours, four nights a week, practicing his rock licks loudly along with his favourite records. He was in several rock bands in the next few years and always had a few gigs every month, but none had any real success. The fun part came, when he bought his own second-hand PA system and started doing some solo gigs in the Shankill and East Belfast, through a local entertainment agent. The UDA and the UVF ran most of these establishments and he was grilled every time while setting up his gear, about where he was from, who he knew and what his own political views were. Billy was careful about how he said things in reply to these questions and he often needed to name drop the top boys from Rathcoole at these venues and pretend he was mates with some of the hardest, scariest guys in Northern Ireland, just so he could safely entertain. He never ever hinted that he was anything less than a 100 per cent 'Orange Protestant'.

Billy's brother, Joseph was a talented drummer and had played in some of the bands with him during this time. Joseph had a mate Stephen, who played a mean bass guitar, but lacked gigging experience. So, Billy and Stephen decided to do a few gigs as a duo to get Stephen the experience he desired and just see how things went, with a view to forming a band in the future. This led on one occasion to a strange night at Suffolk British legion. It was basically a British outpost beside the army barracks at Lenadoon, right in the middle of Nationalist 'Andersonstown'! Billy pulled up in an empty car park and started to unload his gear. With his PA amp under his arm, he announced to the doorman that they were the entertainment for the night. 'That's great son and is that your car out front?' said the doorman. 'It's actually my dad's, Billy casually replied. 'Don't leave it there kid, the fenians on the estate here, chuck petrol bombs and bricks over the fence and they burn any cars parked in our compound. That's why we have a 30ft fence!' 'Fuck me, Billy said, 'Where the hell am I supposed to park then?' The doorman grinned and explained 'Go to the army barracks about 100 yards down the road on the left. Park in the lay-by across the road and shout inside to the soldiers in the gatehouse, that you are entertaining in the British Legion club. The army boys will watch it for you. At the end of the night, just remind them who you are and fetch it back in, load your gear and off you go...Easy, yeh?' 'Christ, I suddenly feel like Custer and the 7th Cavalry, surrounded by the whole fucking Sioux nation!' exclaimed Billy.

He went back into the club feeling a bit bewildered and Stephen just laughed at this whole bizarre set up. They did a good competent set and even reluctantly threw in a few country numbers. Billy always hated Northern Ireland's obsession with Country music. At the end of the night, the small, but very appreciative crowd asked them to come back. Billy coyly said 'Thank you so much, but I really need to speak to our agent'! Outside, Stephen looked at him and said 'Why didn't you just say yes and get us some more bookings?' Billy looked exasperated and said 'Stephen, just think about it! No one else wants to play here, coz' it's like a foreign legion fort in the desert. We are surrounded by hostiles in this place, for God sake. Come on mate, are you not just a wee bit scared in these surroundings. This is enemy territory, any one of those bastards in Lenadoon estate would tear us apart, if they could! Stephen nodded thoughtfully in agreement and said 'Yeah, you are right and it is a bit scary! It's such a shame though, when we just want to play music. That lot really enjoyed us tonight!'

The last couple of gigs Billy and Stephen did together were folk gigs; the first in the Nationalist 'Greenan Lodge', which was quite close to Suffolk British Legion and the second in a Protestant Pub, The Black Bull, just off the Lisburn Road. Billy reminded Stephen to keep his gob shut about politics and they had only a couple of practices at playing this 'compromised' music. They were only used to playing Rock and Blues and were doing quite well until a song called 'Gather up the Pots'. They had rehearsed it so that they each sang the lead on alternate verses, but Stephen's nerves got the better of him and he sung the second verse over Billy's first verse. At the end of the song, the pub manager approached them on stage and Billy immediately thought 'We have blown it, he thinks we are total crap and he is going to tell us to pack up. We couldn't even sing the same bloody words as each other!' As the manager drew level with Stephen, he suddenly smiled and said, 'Good job lads, would you like a drink on the house?' A stunned Billy replied 'Thanks, but I am driving, I'll just have a small coke!' Stephen visibly gulped and gave a shocked smile back at the Manager, then he uttered 'Thanks, I will have a large Jameson's and coke, mate!' They looked at one another in bemused shock.

It appeared that no one in the bar had even noticed the blunder with the lyrics and so they carried on and had a very pleasant evening playing Irish folk songs. At the end of the night, they were approached by a huge drunken man in a Celtic top. He stank of B.O. and booze and growled that he wanted the microphone immediately. He ordered Billy to play 'The Rising of the Moon' on the guitar. Billy did not know this famous Irish rebel song, but on pain of being beaten up, he worked out the Celtic supporter's key and improvised the rest, while this scary individual draped his large, threatening arm around Billy's shoulder. Stephen looked on, concerned for his partner's welfare, but this huge scary man was so drunk that he just managed the one song, before practically falling off the stage, on the way back to his equally drunk and cheering mates. They were both relieved by the time they packed up and left the venue and Stephen vowed not to go back there. The next week, they were just down the road in the Black Bull. They decided to play the same set, as it went down so well in the previous gig. However, about two songs in, a table full of rowdy blokes started to heckle them. 'Can you not play that Fenian crap in here, this is a loyalist bar?' one of them shouted. Billy caught on straight away and started playing 'Streets of London', a well-known English folk song. They followed this with Lindisfarne's 'Lady Eleanor', before the still unsettled crowd shouted out for 'party songs!' Billy looked at Stephen, who had stopped playing and he quietly started to sing the first verse of 'The Sash my Father wore' to the tune of 'Amazing Grace' He shouted to Stephen 'Follow me, It's in G!' He then finished with the full, regular up-tempo version of the song, followed by 'The Orange Lily O', Derry's Walls and the Green grassy slopes of the Boyne. They went down a storm and Billy realised for the first time, just how important it was that every gig should be about playing what music the audience wants and that self-indulgent musicians aren't usually good crowd pleasers.

Back in the tax office, a few days later, Billy was approached by a punk rock friend Paddy McKee. He was an 'up and coming' drummer and had been talking about forming a punk band. Do you want to play as a one-off band, at the office Christmas party? I can get my mate Tommy to play bass and we can do a punk version of White Christmas and I was thinking, maybe the Cars song 'Best Friends

Girlfriend.' This was Paddy's favourite song at the time. Billy thought carefully for a moment and agreed. 'Okay Paddy. You know I am a really a heavy metal and blues man. I am just not into punk music, but as a one off for the Christmas party, it could be good fun! Let's get some gear in and rehearse'. They were allowed a spare room in the office during lunchtimes and spent the next couple of weeks getting the songs off to a good standard.

On the night of the office party, Billy dressed as Mr. Gumbee from Monty Python, with a knotted hanky on his head, as he had no idea how to look like a punk rocker, but he wanted to look unusual and entertaining. They called themselves 'The Bleeding Haemorroids' and did a great, fun performance. The manager was reported to say afterwards 'If they ever get a record deal, they could make Piles!' They won 2nd place in the Talent show behind their 64year-old section manager singing the old music hall favourite 'You made me love You' in her full music hall dancer regalia. She did have the most amazing legs for someone who was near retirement age.

Just as they left the stage, Billy was hit by a thunderbolt. A cute little, smiling brunette was busy distributing sherry trifles among the staff. She came up to where Billy had previously been sitting. He just stared at her in wonderment and couldn't take his eyes off her gorgeous marine blue eyes. ' Paddy, who is she? She's fuckin' lovely 'gasped Billy. 'Take a chill pill will you, Billy; she's Louise Lynch and she works in the Belfast 4 Tax office typing pool!' replied Paddy. For the rest of the night Billy's heart was thumping and his eyes followed this gorgeous vision around the room. He simply didn't have the courage to ask her out.

Billy knew nothing about love, but he pursued Louise off and on the most of the next 4 years. He was besotted and every time he visited the typing pool, his heart nearly bounced out of his chest. In his mind, other girls that he met for years after that, never quite lived up to her standards. He was too thick and naive to see that there was a total world of difference between them and although Louise very maturely grew to love Billy as a friend and they shared many lunch dates, she was simply not interested in 'that' type a relationship with him.

Paddy the Punk became a great friend of Billy's and as he would not compromise his mainstream rock passion, he agreed just to be a Roadie for Paddy's punk band, rather than play in it. The Harp bar in Belfast was where most of the punks played, usually on a Saturday night and Billy cheerfully worked the door over a period of months, despite hating the music. It was a great time for him socially and he got to know a lot of the punk rockers from all over Belfast. His brother Joseph used to occasionally, accompany him and as a drummer, he was often asked to join some of the bands too. Just like Billy, Joseph preferred to play mainstream rock and refused to join any punk band. The one thing Billy never liked was the spitting thing that punks did on each other, when they did their pogo dancing. It was dirty and a possible health risk, but this was all part of their so called 'rejecting society's norms!'

Paddy's band were called 'The Inducers' and they had a gig one night at Donegal Celtic football club, just off the

Andersonstown road, Billy was looking after the gear, as always. He had arrived by bus, as Paddy's dad had delivered all the gear to the venue that afternoon. He had a rather large and useful Volvo Estate car. The Inducers were the only band in Belfast playing Clash covers, at the time. That fact alone meant they attracted a large crowd to their gigs. Paddy went to the bar at the end of the night to get a pint of coke, after a very sweaty gig behind the drums. Suddenly two known local IRA activists approached him and they started a heated argument, as he waited for his drink.

Several weeks earlier Paddy had been involved in a project, sponsored by the BBC to bring Protestants and Catholics together from the opposite ends of the religious divide. It was called the Corrymela project. Paddy had been interviewed as a Catholic and said in front of the television cameras that he liked some of the Protestants he had met, more than some of his Catholic counterparts. One of the IRA men, taking this deliberately out of context shouted ' So Paddy, I hear you like the Proddies more than you like us!'....Paddy instantly and without thinking replied 'Aye, some of them!' Well, this was all the incentive they needed and all hell broke loose as the bouncers tried to hold back the two republicans, while they tried to punch and kick him.

In the middle of this, Billy shouted to Paddy 'What about the gear?' 'Fuck the gear Billy, just get outside!' He watched Tommy and the new guitar player Paul running towards the door. Tommy had his pretty girlfriend Rachel, by the hand. Billy was a hell of a fast sprinter and so as adrenalin kicked in, he rang out of the club and down to the taxi stop at the bottom of the road. There was only one taxi and two startled girls trying to get in it. Billy was usually a gentleman to the fair sex, but he physically hurled the two girls onto the grass verge, with a swift apology, just as his fellow band members reached the taxi. He looked up to see a mob of maybe twenty or so angry republicans bearing down on all of them and noticed also that the two guys who had picked the fight, both brandished large knives. Somehow with the help of the bouncers, Paddy had got out with the rest and he shook himself free from an armlock, just in time to dive into the back of the taxi.

Amazingly, they all managed to get into the taxi and the frightened and obviously stunned driver, drove off instantly with all 'The Inducers' onboard. Ironically, the only casualty was Billy himself, because the taxi window on the passenger side had been opened about 5 inches, wide enough for one of the IRA gang to punch him through it as the taxi moved off. It badly cut him, just above his eyebrow. He needed a few stitches in the Mater hospital, on the way home, but was otherwise just a little shaken.

After that fright and 'lucky' escape, Billy decided he did not want to roadie anymore. His friends managed to retrieve all their music gear two days later, thanks to the club manager refusing to let anyone touch it, on pain of being permanently barred from the club.

A few weeks later Paddy asked Billy to come to his girlfriend's 21st birthday. The only drawback was, the party was going to be in a house, in a street off the Andersonstown Road, again. Paddy reassured him it would be safe, with friends he knew from the band and the other incentive was there might be a few attractive young ladies there too.

On the night of the party, Billy hurriedly left work at 4pm. He went to the Queens Bar, in Fountain street Arcade for a burger and a pint. By 6:30pm he was heading for the Falls Road black taxi rank, with his evening 's supply of beer, to head up to the party. Everyone was there by 7:30pm. The house was packed with young, excited partygoers and Paddy had set up a DJ rig in the living room to get the music going. 'It Should be a fun night,' thought Billy.

Just after 8pm, as the party was getting lively, there was a lot of noise and banging coming from outside. One of the girls started yelling 'Oh, feck...the army are in the front garden'. Billy looked out the window and nearly shit himself. He could see two soldiers crouched behind a hedge in the next garden and watched small pale orange and blazing reddish pink lights shooting past the window. He had never actually seen bullets before and curiously observed that the IRA bullets coming from the flats at the end of the road, were actually a different colour from the SLR bullets from the army. It was terrifying. An IRA gunfight in the street, right outside the party and he was stuck there!

Everyone was paralyzed with fear and without exception they all hit the floor, obviously to minimise the risk from any stray bullets coming through the window. The gun battle raged until after midnight and in the end, there were many army vehicles in the street outside. The partygoers all lay on the floor or hid in the kitchen. No one dared to dance and visits to the toilet meant crawling up the stairs on all fours. Some people huddled together on the floor, awkwardly drinking their bottles of beer and some tried to tell jokes, to relieve the fear. All the while the bullets were cracking away in the dark streets outside. By 2am, all was finally silent outside, but no one dared to venture out. Most of the partygoers, curled up and just fell asleep on the floor where they lay.

At around 6am, Billy woke up on the living room carpet, beside the dim light from the fireplace. 'Paddy, he whispered. 'I got to get out of here! I'm off home, I'll see you at work on Monday!' 'Okay Billy, you take care going home mate!' Paddy nodded. Once the door closed behind him, Billy was suddenly in the middle of a disaster area. Bullets hole through car tyres and windscreens and clumps out of peoples' garden hedges, where the soldiers had been taking cover, the night before. It was a truly frightening scene. It got worse, as he turned into the Andersonstown Road, there were two burnt out single decker buses, three burnt out cars and a taxi, also burnt out, but on its' roof! How did they manage that? In between all of these, were the remains of dozens of petrol bombs and smashed up paving stones. 'Jesus' Billy thought 'We hadn't even realised there was this riot going on around the corner, as last night's gun battle was raging!

He walked slowly and steadily, all the way down the eerily quiet Andersonstown Road and Falls Road into the City centre. It took over an hour, in the early morning residue from last night's unrest! He climbed into a familiar loyalist

black taxi in Bridge Street, heading for Rathcoole and with a deep sigh of relief, made his way home to safety.

Chapter 6:

Existing in troubled times.

The essence of what was happening around Belfast at the time, was the result of a battle of minds between the IRA hierarchy and Margaret Thatcher's government. The hunger strikes had been going on for over 3 weeks, at H Block in the Maze prison and each time one of them died, staged gun battles and riots were the order of the day in all the republican areas. Billy wasn't really interested. He wanted to live his life, play music and go to football. The rest was just a scary inconvenience to him, but he inside he was absolutely terrified of the carnage and murder that was taking place every day.

He constantly worried about becoming another statistic in the Tit for Tat killings in the war between the IRA and the Protestant paramilitaries, but life had to go on. Then he discovered a wonderful place of refuge from all the carnage!... There was only one Rock music club in Belfast in the late 70s, the 'Pound'. It was at the edge of the Nationalist Markets area of the city and so Protestants needed to be careful going there. Once inside the club, it actually didn't matter at all. Rockers were all friends, most of them hated politics and all religious bigotry and just wanted to play or listen to good rock music, get drunk and have a good time. Billy was taken there for the first time, on his 20th birthday by a friend from the Tax office where he worked, and he was completely blown away by a band called Toejam. They were a three piece and played the most amazing version of Zeppelin's Stairway to Heaven, amid a superb set of classic Rock anthems. Someone told Billy that there were bands playing this stuff every week at this venue and so he became hooked.

In the coming weeks and months, Saturdays became Pound music club days. He introduced his Rathcoole friends to his new favourite venue and suddenly the weekends became a straight choice between Liverpool trips and Belfast rock gigs. Local band 'Light' with legendary (ex-Them) guitarist Jim Armstrong, were the Saturday afternoon regulars. They played a lot of their own compositions along with great classic covers such as Layla, Skynyrd's Freebird and Hendrix version of Dylan's 'All along the Watchtower'. His favourite was a rock arrangement of Gershwin's Summertime, as only Jim Armstrong could play it. He used the mouth /fuzz pedal made famous in the 70s by Peter Frampton and loads of echo effects on his guitar. This was like an 'up and coming' guitarist's music lesson and the vastly experienced Armstrong soon became a big influence on Billy's own guitar playing.

Saturday night-time had a completely different feel, in the Pound. The resident band 'Bronco' was a more jazz/rock fusion outfit, led by Armstrong's friend and former band member, Kenny McDowell. They would play the tightest versions of Steely Dan and T Bone Walker songs and Billy loved their amazing version of Runner's 'Run for your Life!'

Billy used to get a bit carried away with the whole rock and roll dynamic, when he went to the Pound. The infa-structure of the building was made with heavy steel girders that looked like railway tracks.

He and his mate Stan thought it was cool to hang off these beams, while headbanging to the music. They did this nearly every week, while the bands were playing. Unfortunately, one Saturday night, a very drunken Billy tried to curl his legs through and spin right over, while hanging off the beam. He relaxed his grip halfway through and landed on the back of his head from a 7ft drop. As a child he had done these spins hundreds of times on school monkey bars, but being drunk, clumsy and older, he was just asking for trouble. He ended up in the Mater Hospital A & E department. He needed stitches and x-rays after a mild concussion and was highly embarrassed on his return to the Pound Club, the following Saturday. It could have had a much worse outcome and thankfully Billy learned his lesson and stopped swinging from the beams after his tumble.

There were some great characters in the Pound Club and none less than Jim Hickson. He wore a long black leather greatcoat, no matter what the weather was like. He had the longest, straightest fair hair of any bloke Billy had ever seen and he used to pull his fingers back through his hair when it fell into his face during conversation. When he told you a story, he always finished with the exclamation 'Seriously!' Jim stood in the same spot every Saturday afternoon drinking pint after pint of coke. Except that it was about 4 years before Billy found out that each pint was in fact a large black Russian. It contained two measures each of Vodka and Tia Maria and then was filled up with coke. He never looked drunk and always coherently and critically analysed each bands performance, at the end of gigs. There were other characters, like the tall curly haired guy who used to get up and do a mad headbanging dance routine in the middle of gigs and then go and sit quietly back in the corner for the rest of the gig. Nobody seemed to know him or what he was called. There was another girl called Anna, who used to bring her baby girl in the pram. She placed a bar chair outside the front door of the club and smoked her head off, while drinking vodka and orange. She loved to hear the music, but she couldn't ever get a baby-sitter. She wasn't allowed to bring a small baby inside the club and although she was careful not to get too drunk; in those days no one checked her for smoking around a baby.

Over the following two years, Billy was persuaded by his friends, to extend his social range by attending occasional disco nights at the local night clubs 'the King Arthur' and 'Ricks'. Being a rocker, he initially hated most of the music, but in time he accepted and even enjoyed the compromise, as they were the best venues to go chasing the fair sex.

One night, Billy's best mate Mark was extremely drunk and threw up all over the back seat of Billy's car. He was mortified the next day and as he worked for an electrical retailer, he promised Billy a new 'State of the art' stereo cassette player for his car, by way of apology. A few nights later, Billy was coming home late from a works darts match and was walking through the Baptist church car park at the end of his street. He suddenly became aware of a sinister looking black car pulling up very quietly behind him. Suddenly, it had full beam headlights flashing and was revving up the engine. Billy froze and was genuinely waiting to be pumped full of bullets. Instead, Mark jumped out of the passenger seat laughing his balls off, as he thrust a brand-new car stereo into Billy's hands. 'You fucking bastard Mark, I thought I was dead! With all the shootings going on in Belfast at the moment, I thought I was a goner!' Mark was totally unapologetic and stood there grinning at his wonderful practical joke. 'The look on your face is priceless, Billy. Enjoy your music and I am sorry again for being sick last week in your car!' He chuckled and left Billy sitting on the kerb and shaking like a leaf, with his new present on his lap. That was just Mark's warped sense of humour!

His friends often took turns driving and staying sober, so occasionally the lads would all head off to the nightclubs in Bangor. Bangor had the Helmsman, The Viking, The Savoy Hotel and the Coachman's. These were all far superior to the clubs in Belfast, but the town of Bangor was regarded as safe for the army and so girls only went there to sample what England had to offer. Billy knew that he and his mates couldn't compete with the muscular mostly 'Black' squaddies. Most of them were incredible dancers for a start. Girls just ignored the local lads, as soon as the soldiers arrived, making visits to these places unproductive, if you were trying to encounter the fair sex. Bangor trips were therefore rare, for Billy and his mates!

As the Branch Organiser for the Tax Office Trade Union, Billy had to attend one of their AGMs, in the Woodlands Hotel at Lisburn. He used to organise the venues, refreshments and entertainment, as part of this role. He heard someone call his name and turned to see an old school friend, Eugene Martin. He didn't have many friends from school, as the hostile Irish Nationalist environment there, severely curtailed his social contact. Although he was a Catholic, Eugene was a bit like Billy and a Unionist sympathiser. He too had struggled with the Republican bullies at school. They began chatting about the days when they had tried to do their GCE O levels during the Ulster Workers strike in 1974. The strike involved a complete commercial shutdown of Northern Ireland and was called because the Unionists believed that too many concessions were being made by the British government to Sinn Fein and the Irish Nationalists. The majority of Ulster Unionists point blank refused to share power with them at Stormont.

This made it difficult for students taking exams and both boys had to be taken to school by their striking fathers each day. All public transport was off for that week, along with electricity and gas. Eugene's father had his car taken off him at a UDA barricade on the third day of exams. He was accused of strike breaking and had to watch it being burned in front of his eyes. He had to recruit the help of a well-connected family friend, to ensure his son got to his History, Science and Mathematics exams, after that.

Billy was much luckier. The Belfast Power Station was completely closed, with no chance to strike break and so when his father Alan, produced his Northern Ireland Electricity Service pass and explained to the armed UDA paramilitaries on the barricade, that his son was doing GCEs and that he was only taking him to school, they were allowed through. There were no buses, so the car was his only option. From then on, the paramilitaries recognised the car and let him through every morning with no problems, until the exams were finished. One of the volunteers on the barricade even used to shout 'What's the subject today then?' Billy also recalled how his mum had stocked up on flour and buttermilk, before the UWC strike. Billy and his dad Alan, had built a temporary stone grate/oven in the back yard, with a metal grill in the middle. Using a cast iron frying pan, Jeanette made Soda bread for the whole street and she did this every day, until the strike was over. A few of the neighbours even gave her extra bags of flour, just in case she ran out!

Billy and Eugene also chatted about how passing the 11 plus exams in primary school, had become a 'Stigmata' to their education and a career hindrance. Most of their friends, who had failed the 11 plus, all ended up doing apprenticeships and got engineering jobs, mainly in Harland and Wolff or Short and Harland Aircraft factory. It seems that grammar school students, who weren't top off the class, mostly ended up with office jobs on less than half of what the engineers earned! So much for a grammar school education! Eugene was currently a Union rep. for Belfast 5 district tax office and coincidentally shared the same clerical officer grade as Billy. They were both glad to resurrect an old friendship and stayed in touch after that.

By 1985, Billy had left the tax office and was selling insurance for the Royal London Mutual. He collected premiums in Monkstown, Rathcoole and Glengormley. These were all tough working-class areas, under paramilitary control. Billy hid his collecting books in two inside pockets of a big baggy overcoat, as he would have been an easy target for gunmen muggers, if they knew he was wandering around collecting money. In the year and a half that he did this job, Billy was lucky never to get mugged. Several of his colleagues in other parts of Belfast, had been held up at gunpoint during this period and had to hand over their takings. All employees were told to pay in their collected funds to the nearest post office, after every two hours of collecting, so that they rarely ever had more than about £50 on them, if anyone did hold them up. They used specifically designed Post Office credit slips for this purpose.

Some of Billy's friends frequented the social club at the Standard Telephone Cables (STC) near Monkstown. He knew a few of the employees there and so was he was able to get an associate membership and have access to cheap alcohol and the weekend cabaret entertainment. It was a much cheaper alternative to going into Belfast city centre. The club had a gym, tennis courts and football pitches too. Sunday nights were particularly busy for live entertainment and Belfast comedian Barry Brent or the variety showband Clubsound, used to completely fill the place. Tickets used to be sold weeks in advance. Billy and his friends had some great times there. He once met an old friend from primary school, Linda Morris. She was due to get married and was with about a dozen girls on her hen night. He kept going over to chat with her, about their childhood in school and how they had both changed so much. By the end of the evening, he was getting on so well with her, that her sister had to intervene and remind her she was on her hen night and she was actually meant to be marrying someone else the following weekend. Billy had been very naughty and snogged her several times on the dancefloor too. He really fancied her!... Maybe she wanted a last fling? Eventually, Linda's sister got her out of the club, before she and Billy got completely carried away and jeopardised her marriage plans!

Ricky a friend from the next street, had just come home on leave from the army after initial training, as a Para. He was in the STC club that same night with Billy and his other mates. Ricky was full of all the arrogance that they teach them on their course and as a dare, he rolled out of an open window, climbed a thirty foot tennis court fence, run round the football pitch twice, climbed back over the tennis court fence and rolled back into the dance hall, before the bouncers even noticed he was gone. He then proclaimed that he wasn't happy with the time it had taken him to complete his task. One of the others had been timing him and he decided to do it all over again, to get under 2 minutes. Ricky and Mark were the best street fighters among their friends and so, when drunken brawls broke out, everyone usually got behind them. The STC was not too bad for fights, but every so often the rival protestant factions would have a bit of a free for all and it would get like a John Wayne cowboy movie. Thankfully, no one Billy knew ever got seriously injured. He himself was regarded as the more intelligent, chilled out pacifist, among his associates. In truth he couldn't fight his way out of a crisp packet.

One Friday night, his friends all went to the Pound Music

club with Paul, another friend on leave from the Royal Navy. Paul did like a fight and when someone shoved him a little too hard at the bar, he started an argument with the bloke. The same bloke went to get support from his mates and a short while later, Paul ended up on a table-top, holding six of them at bay, with a broken beer bottle, while the rest of his mates had a running battle with this other group of lads.

Billy had been at a cousin's wedding that night and missed all the fun, but next morning Mark, Ricky, Paul, Sam and Steve all turned up at Billy's front door. They wildly accused him of not being there to stop the fight and then complained because they had all been barred from the Pound club. 'Hang on!' Billy exclaimed 'You lot are blaming me because you got into a fight, when I wasn't there to calm things down. That is totally not fair and anyway, nobody gets barred from the Pound you stupid pricks. It's a peaceful fun and music loving, you know… 'flower power type' rock club. So what the hell were you all doing and who actually started the fight?' Paul realised it was all his fault and with a bowed head, but an unapologetic wry smile, he verbally apologised to the group. Mark sighed and said 'Well, what do we do now? We won't be allowed back in the Pound for a while!' Billy retorted like a scolding father 'It's your own stupid fault the bloody lot of you. I just hope that they don't bar me too for being your mate! Anyway, did anyone get hurt?' It turned out that Mark had a bruised hand from punching someone, Stan had a slightly swollen lip and Paul did have an unpleasant gash on his back from someone's broken bottle, which resulted in him getting a few stitches and a tetanus jab. 'Well, at least you all seem to be okay!' said Billy 'What about the ones you fought? What are they like?' Stan retorted 'Well, we don't actually know. We didn't hang about to see!'

The group decided to go to the Viking bar that Saturday in the end, as an alternative to the Pound. It was in the City Centre, but a safe distance from the Pound club. Billy went with them to start with, but he was determined to make a point and was planning to go alone, to the Pound club later, as usual. On the way, he decided to look in at Whites Bar, where the guys they had been fighting with usually drank. Sure enough, they were all there. Billy very casually and slowly walked through the bar, as if he was just looking for someone and then he went straight out the back door, after mentally registering their fairly obvious and substantial injuries. He went straight back with haste, to his mates in the Viking. 'Jesus guys, I never knew you lot were such good scrappers! You nearly fucking murdered those poor guys!' Billy gasped, as he hurried in the door. 'What do you mean?' said Mark. 'Well let me see?' said Billy 'One of them had his arm in plaster, one had a large bandage on his head and a black eye. Another had stitches in his face and a bandage on his hand… Oh, and there was one guy on crutches, standing at the bar. That is only the visible injuries! They really look like they have been in a scrap. You guys have hardly a bloody mark on you by comparison and what's more, all the other lot are much bigger than you and they are much scarier looking too. All I can say is, I am glad you are on my side, you mad buggers!'

A few of them had slightly proud looks on their faces. 'Just don't!' sighed Billy, as he waved his finger in their direction. 'Right guys, 'Light' are playing in the Pound, so I am off to enjoy their music, since I seem to be the only one who is not barred. I will see you all later. Be good lads, keep out of fights and don't get barred from anywhere else!' scolded Billy. He got some stares of indignation, particularly from Mark and Paul, but they knew he was right! There were no more fights in the Pound, involving Billy and his mates and after a cooling off period, both groups of lads were eventually allowed back. The music prevailed and as always transcended all barriers. It is a shame that didn't apply to the rest of the political situation in Northern Ireland.

One weekend Billy went off to see a Liverpool/Everton Derby. He was on his own for this one and feeling a bit lonely on the return boat journey, after another depressing 0-0 draw. He started chatting to a pretty redhead from Newry. He liked her look and demeanour and even though she said she was a Catholic, he decided to risk starting a relationship with her. It meant travelling the 50 miles from Belfast to Newry three times a week, but as Billy was ruled by his 'out of control' hormones again, instead of his brain, Billy thought, this girl might be the one! She was called Siobhan. Her family were fine with him straight from the first meeting, as she had introduced Billy as a Belfast Catholic. Technically he was, but it was several months later before he confessed to Siobhan's brother and her cousin while having a beer together, that he was in fact from Protestant 'Rathcoole' and he had stopped attending mass about 10 years earlier. He also admitted to being a converted Presbyterian church goer and a Unionist. As you can imagine, this did not go down well and from that point on, all of Siobhan's family were very lukewarm towards Billy. The old religious bigotry finally raised its' ugly head, when she moved into a flat in a Nationalist estate called Taigowen. On his first visit to her new flat, Billy couldn't fail to notice that every single street had green, white and gold painted kerb stones and Irish Republic flags were tied onto every other lamp post. 'Shit' thought Billy 'this is bloody 'Feniansville'! I am in trouble, if I ever have to live here with her!'

Siobhan went with him one night, to a gig he was playing in the Protestant stronghold of Ballyclare. She asked him not to play 'the Queen' at the end of the night, as she was an Irish Nationalist and found it offensive. Billy thought 'it's only a solo gig, no one will notice, even though he knew he should.' He finished his set around 11pm and as he started packing away, two rough looking guys approached him and quietly said, 'Hey you fucking prick, what are you playing at? If you don't plug your fucking gear back in and play the Queen, you are not going to be allowed to leave here and we will probably wreck you and your gear! This is a proper Loyalist bar and nobody fucks with our traditions right? You are one of us aren't you?' Billy nearly shat himself and stuttered 'Yeah lads, I'm from the 'Coole!' for God's sake. Some of my mates are in the Rathcoole UDA!' The local replied 'So you should know better then, yeah?' He switched all of his gear back on quickly. He then apologised profoundly on the microphone for his neglect of the local protocol and sang the National Anthem enthusiastically, before quietly packing up.

Once outside, he had a blazing row with Siobhan. 'Don't you ever put me in that position again, he said. We could have got our bloody heads kicked in, or worse!' Billy realised that night, that unlike his mum and Dad, he couldn't cope with the religious differences thing, and perhaps Siobhan realised it too.

He had an encounter on another night with Siobhan's brother-in-law, who had been previously an active volunteer for the IRA and had even spent a short time in the Maze prison, for illegally storing weapons and God knows what else? When I say encounter, it was more like a drunken argument, which started over football, but Billy found it hard to be in the company of such an active and verbally bitter enemy of the union and after they had both had a bottle of Buckfast wine each inside them, the inevitable fight broke out. Luckily, Seamus was pulled off Billy by two others in the close vicinity. Billy was definitely not, a fighter, but he had managed a few punches before the fanatical IRA man started to really batter him. Thanks to the guys who broke up the fight, he ended up with only a cut ear lobe and a gash above his eye.

Well, that was the straw that broke the camel's back. He had stupidly spent £500 a few weeks before on an engagement ring, having naively thought that being engaged would somehow, miraculously sort out the differences between him and Siobhan. But now he just had to get out of this poisoned relationship, as soon as possible. Siobhan and Billy sat at the kitchen table in her flat, over a cup of tea and talked about how impossible the relationship was to sustain. There was some love there, but Siobhan expected him to comply with all aspects of her way of life and disregarded all his beliefs, loyalties and desires. She also had a model image in her mind, of the perfect husband, after her first marriage had been unhappy and had involved some domestic abuse. She had accidentally got pregnant at 18 and the Catholic church and her family ensured that the couple did the right thing, against both of their personal wishes, of course. She had far too much baggage for Billy to handle in the long term.

That Sunday afternoon he finally drove home from Newry, with a heavy heart, but he was very definitely a single man again. Siobhan wasn't stupid though! She kept his ring!

Chapter 7:

Just getting on with it!

Billy left his job with the Royal London within a month and decided to go to stay with a friend, in Liverpool. Phil was an Evertonian, who he had met on a work secondment in a Liverpool tax office, five years earlier. In those days Inland Revenue staff from Northern Ireland, were allowed to work in a mainland tax office (most people went to London) for 3 weeks a year, as a break from the stresses of the Belfast troubles. It was all expenses paid and it also gave Billy the chance to see as many home Liverpool games, as he could fit in to a three week period. Over the next five years, Billy got to know Phil's family in Kirkby well and he used to stay over, especially during holiday periods. There were many drunken nights spent in the Liverpool night clubs, Tuxedo Junction, Snobs, the Pyramid club and Tommy Smith's Cabin, often paid for from Billy's work expenses. Billy was also amused that Phil's family were split right down the middle in their football allegiance. His dad was an Evertonian and so was one brother and his sister. Meanwhile the mum, grandmother and other brother were 'Reds'! The football arguments in that house on a Saturday night were incredible. They were all lovely, down to earth and great fun people. Typical Scousers really!

Billy started to go out with a pretty typist Christine, from Liverpool 4 tax office. She picked him up to go on a date to Knowsley Safari Park, one Bank Holiday Monday. It seemed like a novel place to have a date, but it went a bit wrong when Christine's clutch cable snapped in her Ford

Escort, right beside a huge rhinoceros. Billy and Christine sat patiently in the car for over an hour with the rhino getting right up to Billy's car door at one point. He kept muttering 'Is this thing dangerous?' Eventually the ranger came by and using clever positioning of his Land Rover, managed to persuade the rhino to move on. He then casually got out and used a tow rope to get them to the exit from the park. Billy asked the ranger if the rhino could have actually harmed them and he was promptly told that it may have attacked and was more than capable of toppling the car, if they had attempted to get out or been animated too much inside the car. They were right to stay quietly in the car and wait for help!

That relationship didn't last too long either, as Billy got homesick if he was away from Belfast too long. He was a restless and immature spirit, who wanted love, but was too frightened to settle down, if it ever did happen with the right lady.

Billy's friend Sam's sister had gone to live in Canada a few years before. She had married a quiet North Belfast lad called Dennis, who worked hard, liked a pint of Guinness and lived for simple things like Fish and Chips. They had made a good life for themselves in Canada. Sam's youngest sister Stacy was now getting married to Jackie, a Shipyard fitter who was also a drummer with the local orange lodge marching band. Sam asked Billy to come with him to Jackie's stag do. Billy had been singing the night before at a pre-wedding house party in Jackie's Dad's and so the invitation had come from Jackie himself.

They were both charged by Sam's mum to make sure that Jackie got back home safely, if the lads from the band got too drunk and caused trouble. She knew what they were like, when they all went out drinking.

It was a Sunday evening and they had booked to go to Rothmans Carreras club, in the Tobacco factory in Carrickfergus. One of the group owned a 12 seater minibus and squeezed 16 of them into the bus to head down to the club. At the first road junction they had to stop for a church parade. It was the local Orange lodge marching behind a very dignified looking accordian band, playing 'Onward Christian Soldiers'. Suddenly, one of the lads on the bus shouted out 'Let's pretend we are Fenians and wind these bastards up!' They all started shouting and singing IRA songs out of the windows of the bus. Within seconds, the bowler hat brigade in the church parade, started beating the side of the minibus with their umbrellas and members of the accordian band were pelting it with stones. The driver took the party out of it quickly and amid hilarious laughing on the bus, from the instigators, Billy noticed that Sam's brother-in-law, Dennis had a look of total terror on his face. He shouted across to him 'Dennis, this is just a bit of fun for this lot. They are all as hard as nails. You were never in any danger!' Dennis was not used to this kind of thing anymore, after his years living in peaceful Hamilton, Ontario. Billy knew that this was going to be a mad night.

Inside the large social club, they agreed everyone should put cash into the 'kitty' for beer and two of the lads quickly took care of the first order. After a few pints Billy looked around and reminded himself that he was now drinking with some of Rathcoole's hardest/toughest characters. How did he ever manage to shake of the 'Wee Fenian' image and get to this stage? It felt so good to be just one of the boys, but scary too, because of their fierce reputations. He was ordered by one of them, to take his shirt off. Everyone in the party had to strip to the waist. The bouncers immediately moved in to see what was going on. Ronnie Lorimer was the main man. He stood up and rebuked the bouncers' challenge. 'There are six of you and including the ones who made their own way and met us here, about twenty of us. We just want to give Jackie a fun stag do, so if you don't interfere, we won't cause you any trouble for you. None of us want the Razzers (Police) here!'. Despite the slightly alarming look of twenty or so, shirtless blokes in one corner of the club, this seemed like a good arrangement for just that one night. The bouncers were mindful of the type of people they were dealing with too. So the night continued tentatively and at one point, Billy spotted his friend Eric that he had played guitar with in a band, sitting with his wife. They were right at the opposite end of the hall. He sat down to chat to them, as the cabaret started. The band was one of the top showbands in Belfast at the time. The lead singer, Trevor Scott thought he was Ireland's answer to Frank Sinatra and so he was cockily strutting his stuff, in front of the Sunday night crowd of about 300 plus. Eric suddenly stared with disbelief at Billy, who at this point had his back to the stage. He shook his head and said despairingly, 'Billy, look at what those fucking pricks you came in with are doing now!' Billy turned around and there were four of the shirtless wonders carrying Jackie above their heads. He was totally naked, pissed out of his brains and shaking his manhood, as they walked, grinning all the way across the front of the stage, right in the gap on stage, between the band and the singer. They then paraded all the way round the hall with their naked exhibit, to loud gasps, mainly from middle aged ladies. The bouncers were livid and once again confronted Ronnie. The head bouncer shouted, 'Ronnie, this is not what we agreed. We will have to call the cops, if you don't cool this stuff down right now! It's about public decency, right?' Ronnie was quite pissed by this stage, but he did nod in agreement and apologetically told his lads to calm it down, for the rest of the night. It could have got very scary in the club, otherwise.

At the end of the evening, as soon as they were all outside the heavy security gate, the bouncers shouted to them 'You lot are all barred, we have you all on CCTV. So, don't bother coming back!' Billy could not believe that it was his first visit to maybe the best Working Men's club in Northern Ireland and it was to be his last. He climbed back into the small minibus and now 16 people had suddenly become about 32. People were literally sitting and lying across or on top of each other and the journey home was going to be uncomfortable. There were also about 4 girls in the company now, too. One of the girls started to shriek playfully in the dark, as one of her male friends started to get amorous. The next thing, a pair of bright yellow lacy panties were being tossed around the minibus in the darkness. Billy even put them on his head at one point, before someone grabbed them and flung them back down the bus. A few minutes later another of the lads put them in his pocket to keep as a souvenir. There wasn't actually any room for any hanky-panky and that was probably a good thing, as it could have got really silly. Dennis still had the same worried look on his now drunken face, as he had earlier in the evening and he just couldn't wait to get out of the minibus. He didn't seem to have enjoyed much of the evening. When they did stop, Billy was one of about eight people, who tumbled out the back door and he was lying on the road laughing, as others climbed over him, trying to stand up. He shouted to the girl 'Did you get your knickers back, love?' but she ignored him as everyone went their separate ways. Sam dusted Billy and Dennis off. 'Right, are we all okay? Come on, I need a cuppa' tea, to sober up!' They started walking towards Sam's house. He had forgotten his key and so he had to knock the door. Sam's mum stood there and just stared hard at the three drunken reprobates standing at her front door. 'Have you lot forgotten something?' She said. 'Nah' Sam retorted, as they all tried to push past her into the house. 'So where is Jackie then, you know, my youngest daughter's intended? You promised me you would bring him home safely?' The three lads stared at each other in disbelief and Billy gasped 'Oh fuck guys, we left Jackie behind. In fact, now that I think about it, he wasn't even with us on the bloody minibus!'

Dennis spoke for probably the first time all night, 'Imagine, we have been to a stag do and forgot to bring the groom home!' Sam's mum was so angry and was ready to batter the three of them. She verbally tore them to pieces for their irresponsible attitude. She particularly looked at Billy and scolded. 'I know my son is a bloody idiot, but I thought you were more responsible William!' Billy felt like a little naughty schoolboy getting told off by the teacher. It was about 1am, but after about twenty minutes of phone calls, they eventually located Jackie's whereabouts. Ronnie Lorimer had him tucked up in his spare room, drunk and asleep. Everyone breathed a sigh of relief and Billy went home.

After the Inland Revenue and the Royal London, Billy was struggling to get work at home. He worked briefly in a pub in Glengormley, close to home, called the Ski Lodge. It looked like a Swiss Ski Lodge, but was just another themed pub. The problem was that the owner deliberately paid staff only £1.50 an hour and actively encouraged them to claim dole at the same time. It was illegal, of course and the landlord knew exactly how to cut his staffing costs, but Billy, just like the rest of the staff, was desperate for the work. He worked there for a few weeks and befriended a pretty girl from his own Rathcoole. Josie wouldn't go on a date with Billy, but she admitted to liking him a lot. As they got closer, he kept asking her why and then she told him; She had been going out with a married UVF gunman for nearly a year. He was using her for sex and she knew it, but was too frightened to get out of the relationship. He was quite a violent man and had already suggested that he might have Billy killed, if he kept seeing Josie in his company. Billy soon left the pub and left her, for his own safety. He felt a deep sadness, as they could have been a great couple in different circumstances. His next job was ironically at the local dole office on a six-month contract, as they changed over from the old Supplementary Benefit system to the new Jobseekers allowance. He had been signing on one afternoon and the Benefits officer told him, as she perused his records, that they were looking for temporary staff. Billy's previous experience in the Tax office, made him a prime candidate. A few weeks after starting work there, Billy heard that Josie had been up in court and received a suspended sentence for her part in hiding illegal weapons for the married boyfriend. The boyfriend got 6 years in jail, for this and several other charges. Billy was well out of that situation, although he felt that in different circumstances, he and Josie could have had a very meaningful relationship.

While working in the local DHSS, he had to sit with a team of about a dozen workers. Their job was to prepare new folders and records for every one of the local benefits claimants and they all got to be friends, from working in close proximity. A young couple in this group, were noticeably very much in love but spent most of their time talking about the bible and their local church in Greenisland, the Church of the Nazarene. They introduced him to another staff member and friend, called Joanne. She was also a member of their church and since Billy fancied Joanne, he had to attend her church, in order to get her to go out with him. Billy had always hated the narrow-minded Bible thumpers in Rathcoole, but he decided that maybe they knew something after all and it was worth giving it a go. So, he threw himself into the church. He read his bible and prayed every day. Billy was finally persuaded that he had been 'Saved' at one point, during an intense prayer meeting with a group of these Nazarenes. They built up deep emotionalism with bible readings, prayer and singing. After about twenty minutes of this, the intensity got so deep that Billy felt he wanted to cry with joy and it really was a joyful and uplifting experience. All the participants had had this before and kept saying that the Holy Spirit was working in him and that he was now saved. The euphoria was amazing, but Billy was still suspicious of his new-found zeal for God. Some people might explain all this as a form of mass self-hypnosis. It felt great at the time. That is all that mattered to Billy.

In the following weeks, Billy got closer to Joanne and attended the Nazarene church at least twice a week. They even held prayer fellowships in each other's houses on weeknights. At one of these, a church member even loudly thanked Jesus for saving Billy from his past life in the misguided clutches of the Catholic church. Billy carefully observed the practices of these dedicated churchgoers and while he respected their views, he soon realised that they had certain intolerances that he didn't agree with, such as towards gay people, sex outside marriage, alcohol and swearing. They chose to live in a Utopian bubble of their own making, that excluded so much of the interesting, intriguing and diverse aspects of life. When Joanne's mum, on one occasion wrote a letter to Ian Paisley about advice on a church matter, Billy suddenly realised that these people were just as insecure as he was, in their faith. While he respected Paisley, as a charismatic politician, Billy disagreed with much of his religious doctrine and interpretations of the Bible. He found it a little disturbing that Joanne's mum needed advice from such a controversial figure. There were also several instances in the church where people had arguments and differences of opinion, as people do, but the Pastor and Joanne's mum insisted these instances was the devil working amongst them and that they all should pray away these evil threats to church unity.

Billy thought 'Wow, that is an overreaction...this is fear speaking, not religious faith!' Billy concluded that these lovely people didn't know any more than him after all. He preferred to keep an open mind, than to simply accept the seemingly one dimensional attitude they all had towards God, the Bible and to life. He was deeply disappointed in the end, that his new friends couldn't offer him that deep sense of religious redemption and comfort, he had always searched for.

He had had a fall out with his mother about his church going and the time he spent every day reading his bible. It was unpleasant and hurt them both, as the Church were saying it was unhealthy for him to be around papist beliefs and he should not even be living under the same roof as someone with an opposing religious viewpoint. In a eureka moment, Billy suddenly realised his new religious fanaticism had hurt one of the people he loved most in the world and when he thought about the apparent inconsistencies in the Church of Nazarene teachings, he decided to stop going. He finally escaped the religious life, when he was offered a job for the summer in Portimao, on Portugal's Algarve coast. Joanne begged him not to go, but he had always wanted to play his music abroad and the pull was just too strong.

A few weeks later, Billy arrived in Faro airport with a backpack and two guitars. It was about 3 am and the lady who had promised to meet him, wasn't there. He used an airport phone box to ring her. She was the entertainment coordinator at the place where he was due to work. She had been very busy that night and couldn't manage to get to the airport to pick him up. She apologised for leaving Billy stranded in the middle of the night and told him what bus he needed to get to Portimao, in the morning. He couldn't speak any Portuguese and he now needed somewhere to crash for the night. Billy started to wander around the small airport arrivals hall. An airport security man, who could speak a little English, told him he could not stay there and after a short conversation, he felt sorry for Billy's predicament. He said his name was Jose and he quickly rang his Aunt, who lived in Faro town. He then drove Billy in his own car to the lady's small, terraced house, not far from the Airport. Billy thanked Jose for all his trouble. The Aunt, who was called Josephina gave him a comfy bed for the night, in her spare room. He paid her about 250 escudos (just a couple of pounds in those days) for the night and she even gave him coffee and a croissant in the morning, before he left. She was a very kind lady, even though they couldn't converse properly and Billy thought to himself, that if this was an example of Portuguese hospitality, he was going to have a great time there.

Two and a half hours later, finally Billy arrived at the Dennis Inn in Portimao, by bus. It was a very hot morning in July and still only around 10:30 am. He met the entertainment coordinator, Donna O'Reilly.

She was a hard-nosed, no nonsense Derry girl and had an accent that could cut glass. She led him to the staff quarters, in a tenement style building, two blocks away from the pub. She was a typical Northern Irish catholic, of course and seemed a little bit uneasy with Billy being from Rathcoole. He was then introduced to three boys and three girls that he would be sharing with. Marie and Sean were a couple from Dublin and they both worked the bar. Mary was a singer from Dublin and did some great versions of Whitney Houston songs. Brendan and Rory were both singer/guitar players from Cork and then there was Molly who was from a well to do farming family in Co. Wicklow. She helped Donna with all the catering and organising the entertainment. For the first time in his life, Billy had a chance to mix with real Southern Irish people and to see if he could get along with them. Over the next six weeks, each singer worked on a rota basis. They each did half hour spots, performing every evening in the restaurant. If there were four entertainers on a particular night, they would have each done 3 spots by midnight, when the bar closed. The music started at 6pm each night and it was always a case of playing quiet background music and ballads, while people were eating until around 10pm. Then it was cranked up to an entertainment level with singalong Irish folk and rock songs, to create a proper holiday atmosphere, until around midnight.

Brendan taught Billy a lot about Irish folk music, including pentatonic jigs and dance tunes and Billy just fell in love with Mary's voice. In fact, he fell in love with the rest of her too, but couldn't do anything about his feelings, as she kept enthusing about her fiancé back in Ireland. She was a class act and her claim to fame a few years later, was that she sang as a backing vocalist for Johnny Logan at Eurovision. The Dennis Inn was a lively bar and restaurant in the centre of Portimao and was owned by a French-Canadian couple, Jacques and Louise. They loved having Irish singers working for them and as Louise was a big Beatles fan, everyone had to include a lot of Beatles songs in their repertoire.

The pattern of existence for the next few weeks consisted of singing between 6pm and midnight in the restaurant, six nights per week, then heading up to the beach at Praia da Rocha to the Man of Arran. This was an Irish music pub and stayed open until 4am each night. There were usually quite a lot of local musicians there and all the Dennis Inn crowd used to get up on stage and jam with them and the resident band, who were an Irish folk trio. Needless to say the beer and whiskey was flowing in large quantities too. On return to the digs, they all managed 4 or 5 hours sleep and hangover permitting, they went back to the Dennis Inn for a free breakfast. The wages were basic, but the accommodation and food was provided by the pub Management, so it was quite a good deal really.

Most days saw the Dennis Inn staff sitting together on the beach by 11:30am and they lay there sunbathing till about 5pm. After a shower and some food, the cycle began again by 6pm. Portimao Sardines are among the biggest and best in the world and so Billy acquired a taste for them. The fish Restaurant close to the Dennis Inn, was one of the best in all Portugal, or so they claimed. Billy also experienced authentic Fado (Portuguese traditional music) music. This was by invitation only, in back street venues and was definitely not accessible to philistine tourists. The music itself had a Spanish flamenco feel, but with some African style rhythms and some complex jazz style chord structures. On one occasion, Billy watched in awe as a Moroccan percussionist kept them all entertained for about twenty minutes, with just a pair of bongos. He was about 30, with a completely bald head and had the blackest skin that Billy had ever seen. The talent of the man was simply amazing and it made Billy look critically at his own performance skills. This place was music and cultural heaven!

In all his time in Portugal, none of Billy's new Southern Irish friends got into any arguments with him about Northern Ireland politics. He thought this was incredible. They said that actually they felt sorry for anyone from the North, but him being a Protestant, was no big deal to them and they seemed to like Billy for who he was. It appeared that it was only the Provo fanatics in the North, who seemed to be pushing for a United Ireland. The real Irish people just wanted to live in peace and found it all a political irritation!

Donna made everyone in the staff residence, a huge Bolognese one night, for tea. She went to a lot of trouble to make it a nice evening, with wine and cake for afters. It seems that the meat she had bought that day in the market, may have been slightly off or contained certain additives that put everyone into some-kind of a sickly depressive mood. The atmosphere felt strange after the meal, like they had all been drugged. Billy just had to get out and he quickly followed Molly to what was the only night club in Praia da Rocha, at the time. They flirted briefly and he kissed her, but she wasn't stupid and told him that she knew he really fancied Marie. Marie was with Sean of course and so Billy's next target for his affections had to be Mary, the lady with the Whitney Houston voice. Molly was really clued up on who fancied who and she warned him that Mary's fiancé was arriving the next day from Dublin and so he had no chance there either. Billy liked Molly a lot. She was a strong gutsy lady, but he didn't fancy her at all. They actually became good friends instead.

Craving other female company, Billy decided to ask the visiting travel rep. Katherine out on a date. They got on well and he had a few dates with her, during his time in the Algarve. They even played a doubles tennis match one afternoon, with their Entertainments director, Donna and her boyfriend. That same evening, they all left the Dennis Inn just after midnight. Brendan was walking with the four of them. Suddenly a small motor bike with two riders, came flying up the street towards them. Brendan pushed Donna out of the way, as the bike came level with them. He thought it was about to knock her down. The bike slowed right down and suddenly the pillion passenger wrestled Katherine's bag from her shoulder, before anyone could stop them and they sped off into the night. Billy and Brendan instinctively pursued the motor bike through the narrow, winding streets of Portimao. After about half an hour of running around, they gave up and went to the town's police station. The incident had happened so quickly that no one managed to get a registration for the bike. The Portugese police logged the incident, but they said that they would not be able to retrieve Katherine's bag without some kind of a lead, descriptions of the criminals or the bike's registration. She lost money, make up and her credit card, which she quickly cancelled, but thankfully she had left her passport in her room. It was a harsh lesson quickly learned and all the girls made sure that they carried their bags across their bodies from that point on.

At the end of his six-week stint, Billy decided to travel back to Britain by coach and ferry. He had all his gear with him in the Man of Arran, the night before and drank till 4am. He went to the coach pick up point outside Portimao for 7am, at which time he was still quite drunk. It was understandable, as his friends had bought him a lot of drinks, since they were saying goodbye. After about an hour into the coach journey, Billy felt hot and quite sick. He threw up all over the floor, under his seat and the summer heat made the smell overwhelming. Two understandingly irate Portuguese ladies in the seat behind, gave Billy some very cross stares. A little while later the coach stopped for a break. He asked the driver, if he had time, to let him fetch a bucket of disinfectant from the services café. The driver was only too happy to let Billy clean up his own mess. Using a mop, he disinfected the whole area around his seat and the smell improved immediately. He apologised to the two ladies behind, when they returned to their seats and after consuming about 2 litres of water and eating a cheesy croissant, Billy suddenly felt alive again. It took two coach changes, lots more stops through Salamanca and Santander in Spain and Paris in France and then the Dover ferry, before Billy eventually arrived in London Victoria coach station. It was exactly 48 hours after he began his journey. He was met by his scouse friend Phil, who let him stay with him overnight in Colliers Wood, near Wimbledon. He even loaned Billy the cash to book his trip back to his home in Belfast. It had been another interesting adventure, with more life lessons learnt.

Chapter 8:

Family Troubles

Billy's sister, Anne had passed her 11 plus. This was a big deal back then and She then was accepted into the Catholic Convent (grammar) school at nearby Fortwilliam. Her school was unfortunately, just across the road from the local Protestant Comprehensive and so it became a flashpoint for sectarian bullying, during the troubles. Anne had to cope every day with stone throwing, name calling and even being kicked, tripped up and spat at, as she tried to walk past or through the students from the rival Protestant school. She also had to cope with the same at the nearby bus stops and often would have to keep walking up to three bus stops away, before she felt safe enough to get on one.

She pleaded with Mum and Dad to get her out of this insane daily battle and back to the Star of the Sea Secondary school in Rathcoole. Anne also claimed that the nuns were bullying fascists and that there was a group of weird students at the convent, who were experimenting with the occult. They quickly moved her back to the local school, who were only too glad to take her, as a potential high-quality student, due to her 11plus grade. Although it was not as highly regarded as the Convent school, she felt much safer and happier. She didn't seem to get bullied very much, walking home from her new school either.

Billy's brother Joseph, went to Star of the Sea Secondary School too, as it was mixed gender and more relaxed than the outdated, but still prevalent, strict regimes of single gender and single faith grammar schools. Anne achieved some quality grades and did really well at the school. Joseph, on the other hand, had some learning difficulties that they didn't bother to diagnose in those days. He struggled through school, even though he didn't quite experience the level of bullying that his older siblings had.

Anne used her qualifications to go off to London at 17, to train as a State Registered nurse. She was sick to death of the Northern Ireland troubles by then and was glad to get away. She also had an older cousin in the same London Hospital, who had already succeeded as a nurse and she used her as her inspiration. Joseph spent a long time on the dole after school, but he put this time to good use learning oil painting and developing his skills as a drummer/percussionist. By the 1980s, he was in 5 bands, all at the same time and was well known locally, as a top Reggae and Rock drummer. His natural artistic skills came to the fore, as his paintings received local acclaim and in the 1990s, as a mature student, he finally earned himself an Art degree at Ulster University.

Billy's youngest sister Agnes was 8 years younger than him and so he always felt ultra-protective to her. He remembered his mum Jeanette saying that when she brought Agnes home from hospital as a baby, Billy wouldn't leave the side of her cot for weeks. By the age of 17, he was working constantly and was always off on his Liverpool trips. Agnes was about 9 years old at around the height of the troubles. She often had to go to school and sit in a blackened classroom. She was often freezing cold and had to keep her coat on, until they replaced the glass in the windows. The smell of burnt wood and melted plastic was constantly in her nostrils, even when she got home. The reason for all of this, was that nearly every weekend the local Protestant Youths would throw stones and petrol bombs over the school fence, at the school buildings and they almost succeeded in burning the school down completely on two separate occasions. It was a constant rebuild and repair situation, as these relentless delinquents unfairly ravaged the little Catholic Primary school. It didn't matter how high they built the fence, the petrol bombs and bricks always got through and did their damage. Agnes and all her classmates suffered severe trauma from all of this. It was appalling that the RUC wouldn't protect these young children from this mindless vandalism. Nobody bothered with CCTV camera or patrols in those days. The Police said they didn't have the resources, but it was more likely this was a blatant act of discriminatory neglect by them? Somehow Agnes had to accept and deal with all this hatred, fear and violence around her every day. She was only 9 for God's sake! Billy wasn't always there for her, as he was so busy with his frantic, fun lifestyle. It was inevitable that she resented him for always being away, when she needed her big brother most.

Ironically Agnes, Anne and Joseph had all wished they could have gone to the local Protestant schools and just be allowed to fit in. All three of Billy's siblings hated and abhorred the IRA and the 'Hitler youth' style behaviour of the Nationalist supporters poisoning the Catholic schools. Outside of school, each of them spent every day trying to convince suspicious friends and neighbours, that they weren't stereotypical Catholics. The Nationalists were in fact only a small group in school, but most teachers never dared to challenge them, due to the nature of the political and paramilitary activities of their families. The teachers feared that to speak out would perhaps put their own lives in danger.

Billy's dad Alan had made a promise to the Catholic Canon in 1957, that he would allow the kids to be brought up Catholic. This promise had come back to haunt the family. Jeanette had always been terrified to disobey the strict code of the Catholic Church, but often wished she had allowed her children to go to the Protestant schools. Life simply would have been much easier for them all, especially at the height of the troubles. Despite the awful trauma and horrors of being constantly taught in a bombed-out school, Agnes was quite a clever student, particularly in English. She later used her impressive literary skills to get into journalism and worked for several media companies, including the BBC. She later turned to PR work with Belfast ship builders, Harland and Wolff. Jeanette was just pleased that all her children had managed, at least a semblance of a career, despite the constraints and constant disruption of the Troubles.

In August 1972, when Billy was about 14, he looked up at his bedroom window from the garden and thought 'the ledge above the living room window is about 6 inches wide; it's also about 8 feet off the ground and if I climbed out my bedroom window, I could ease myself down onto that ledge.

I could then jump into the garden and roll forward to break my fall without hurting myself!'... So, he did! The only problem was that as he landed, he didn't roll forward on impact and his knee glanced off his chin on landing. He cut the bottom of his tongue slightly with his teeth, due to the impact, but he did the jump again. This time he rolled onto his side like a parachute jumper. Billy was feeling very pleased with himself at the outcome of his outrageous self-challenge. It was a typical silly and dangerous stunt for a bored teenager to do, on a summer afternoon. Jeanette got quite angry with Billy and started to lecture him about injuries and hospital visits, etc.

A week later at around 3am on a Sunday morning, Billy was awakened by his mum, Jeanette shouting 'The bloody house is on fire, get out quickly, all of you!' She managed to get the girls and herself out through thick smoke, but Joseph was coughing and struggling desperately in the bedroom doorway, trying to get through the smoke to the staircase. Billy was choking too, but quickly pulled Joseph back by the collar of his pyjama top. 'Come on Joseph, we can climb out of the bedroom window. I know how to do it! Just do as I tell you and we can jump safely into the garden. I have already done this just last week, as a challenge!' Despite the now heavy smoke, Joseph and Billy climbed out carefully onto the ledge above the living room window and they both jumped safely, remembering to bend their knees to the side on impact. Luckily, it had been raining earlier and the grass was wet and muddy. The soft, wet ground helped to break their fall. Ironically, Billy's idiotic stunt the week before, had probably saved their lives. Alan was last one out of the house, but all were okay, apart from mild smoke inhalation. The fire brigade arrived in a short space of time and quickly contained the fire, in the living room area. The local UDA boss appeared, as if on cue. He looked at a bewildered Alan, standing in the street. 'If this is our lot, they are fucking dead!' He thought the fire had been caused by petrol bombs and that they were being victimized because of the mixed religion thing. He also knew that the family were decent people and Loyal unionists at heart. None of it was relevant, as the Fire Chief assessed the situation quite quickly, after the fire was extinguished. The cause of the fire had been an ember of coal jumping out from an improperly guarded fire and had landed on the huge Chesterfield settee, setting it alight almost immediately. The asbestos in the ceiling structure had apparently saved them from a ceiling collapse and from getting burned to death. The charred remains of the settee lay on a patch of grass in front of the house. You could clearly see the centre of it was burnt, almost completely and only the blackened arms and a few springs were left.

That summer, they all struggled to watch the Olympics on the old melted valve television, with its very dodgy frame hold. The weightlifting never looked so funny and the swimmers all appeared to have double the lanes. Agnes made it funnier, as she stood in front of the telly, twisting her head to the side and following the moving frame hold up and down the screen.

Billy's mates enjoyed the novelty of playing their Subbuteo table soccer league matches, in the burnt-out living room, taking turns with a hand-held unshaded lamp for floodlighting. They also had to be careful to avoid a 4foot wide and 3foot deep hole in the floorboards. Thankfully, this was fixed within a week by the local Housing Executive. It took many months to gradually get the house redecorated and back to normal, despite daily help from the neighbours. It was suddenly apparent that after many years of lukewarm acceptance, they were now rallying with vigour and overwhelming generosity. The McCrees were definitely accepted as 100 per cent 'Rathcoolians' from that day on.

Raymond and Geordie, Billy's neighbours and friends, built a hut in Raymond's backyard from unused bonfire wood from the 11th July that had just gone. They lined the walls with football pictures and decided to camp out in the very fragile building. Billy asked his mum, who agreed to let him sleep in the hut, but she warned him to behave and not to go running around the estate in the middle of the night, annoying the neighbours. Unfortunately, Geordie was a bit of a mischief. Not a bad lad really, but he did like the challenge of some petty theft on occasions. That night, while camping out, Geordie persuaded Billy to go on an expedition with him, for lemonade and crisps. He explained to Billy that the local mobile shop owner used a coal shed, instead of a lock up, where he stowed his stock of lemonade, crisps and cleaning agents. Geordie had his own tools, including a massive screwdriver, which he intended to use in the middle of the night for a break in. Raymond told them both, they were mad and wanted nothing to do with this. He looked dismayed and said, 'Don't get fucking caught!' and continued to sleep the night away proudly, in his self-built hut. At around 4am, Geordie and Billy went out to the targeted shed. It was getting light and so they had to be extra careful, without the cover of darkness. Billy kept watch and Geordie skilfully undid the screws in the very basic lock. The next minute, they were both running up the street with a crate of lemonade each and two large boxes of crisps on top. For weeks after, the shop owner quizzed people coming into his shop about the missing lemonade and crisps. He never suspected Billy, but Geordie had previous form and the owner had no proof, but basically told him he would never be welcome at his shop again. Geordie was indignant that the robbery wasn't his work, but it seems that several local people strongly hinted they had seen him brazenly walking around for about 3 days in a row, drinking nothing but pineappleade, of all things. He was noticeably munching multiple packets of Tayto Cheese and Onion, on each occasion too. Whoops!

Most people have happy memories of their grandparents, but Billy and his siblings all agreed that they had no genuine affection for their grandfather Robert McCree. He was perpetually grumpy and Victorian in his attitudes. When they were little, Billy, Anne, Joseph and Agnes all remembered having to sit quietly, palms of hands turned outwards, between closed thighs, for up to three hours on their Saturday visits. Granda McCree religiously watched the wrestling on World of Sport. He loved Mick McManus and Big Daddy. Billy was always restless and after about an hour, he would start wandering around the living room, picking up ornaments and being an inquisitive nuisance. Granda had a little ornamental brass bell on his window-sill and Billy used to sneak a teaspoon from the kitchen drawer and start hitting the the bell with it. Granda McCree never swore, as he was a devout Protestant, but my God he used to lose his temper with Billy. It always ended with Alan yelling at Billy and sending him out for a walk on the Donegal road to cool off.

Billy loved this and used to wander up to Windsor Park football ground or watch the steam trains near Tates' Avenue bridge. It was obvious that their Granda still regarded his grandchildren as horrible little fenians and only tolerated them because of his son. Billy's siblings had to just sit there like zombies until Alan decided it was time to go. Years later Joseph told Billy he always thought he had been sly to get sent out and not take him with him.

Saturdays generally meant family shopping on the Shankill Road, followed by their visit to their Granda's and then driving back across the religious divide to the Falls Road to visit Granny Cameron (Jeanette's mum). She was constantly moving house. She lived in the old kitchen houses at Gilford Street, off the lower Falls Road in the 60s, then the infamous Divis flats in the early 70s, during the troubles. She moved later to old people's flats at Shaw's Road in Andersonstown and even had the audacity to move close to Jeanette in Protestant Rathcoole for a year, before eventually ending up in back in her birthplace, the little village of Whiteabbey. The woman was unbelievably restless and demanding. Jeanette had her work cut out running after her needs. Granny Cameron was generous with money, but she had no concept or understanding that her daughter was working every day and also trying to bring up 4 children, while running after her also. She also had a short memory, as she couldn't be bothered to be a proper mother to Jeanette, when she was a child and had left her two aunts to bring her up. That fact was not lost on Billy, who respected his grandmother, but had only a mild affection for her. Their other grandmother had died when Billy was 3. She was reputed to be a real lady and a warm human being. How ironic that Billy never got to know her.

Granda Cameron, had died when Billy was just 3 months old and so he never knew him either. Apparently, he died of a heart attack after listening to Northern Ireland's World Cup quarter final in 1958, on the radio. They were battered 4-0 by France. He had a heart condition and wasn't supposed to get excited. He had been a Belfast Celtic supporter up until 1948, when the club was disbanded due to sectarian tensions with the local Protestant team Linfield. They were based a mile away from Celtic Park, at Windsor Park and so the area was a hot spot for religious hatred on match days. Remember, this was 20 years before the Troubles! Jeanette always said that Billy got his genetic passion for football from his Granda. He was quite a character and as an old soldier, who had frequently guarded King George V, he would not have had any time for the Irish Nationalists of Billy's day. He also believed that a man was not a man, if he didn't take a drink and he thought it strange if someone didn't like football.

The best story about Granda Cameron was the one Jeanette used to tell about how in 1921, he was home on leave from the army. There had been some civil unrest in the Falls Road and the newly recruited Black and Tans were supposed to be helping the Police deal with troublesome republican sympathisers. They pulled him in while walking alone down his own street and were about to shoot him, as a suspected republican sympathiser, when a local regular policeman turned the corner and hurriedly vouched for him as a serving British soldier, who was definitely not a Republican. He even showed his dog tags, at which point the Black and Tan soldier lowered his weapon. Billy often thought if they had shot his granda, then his mother would not have been born, nor would he or his siblings! It made him think how taking just one life always carries the risk of a terrible domino effect on others.

It was impossible for anyone living in Northern Ireland in the 1970s and 1980s, not to be affected by the Troubles. Billy didn't like to dwell on his fears, but he did lose a schoolmate when he was 12, due to a terrorist bomb. It felt creepy, seeing the television news cameras, as they filmed their whole school yeargroup in full uniform, at his friend's funeral. His dead classmate had been playing Subbuteo with the bar manager's son, on the previous Saturday evening, in a room above McGrath's Bar. It was a popular bar in the North of Belfast. No one knew if the bomb had been planted by the IRA, as punishment for the manager not paying protection money, or if a Loyalist group had planted it, in retaliation for protestants being shot earlier in the week, in 'drive by' shootings! This was now at the height of the Troubles! Another of his old schoolfriends' lost his legs in another pub bomb in the late 1970s and one of his cousins on the Nationalist side of the family, joined the IRA and was accidentally killed along with two other Provo volunteers, when a planned bombing went wrong and they blew themselves up. Billy refused to attend his cousin's funeral, as he knew the IRA would hijack it for their show of propaganda, apart from despising his cousin's political views. He was right. His mother came home in a very traumatised state, after witnessing the volleys of shots over the coffin, the black masks and all the sinister paraphernalia. They even invited television cameras to milk the situation for their propaganda purposes. His cousin James had been beaten up several times by the army patrols on the Falls Road. He had built up hatred for them after his beatings and the IRA propaganda machine had persuaded him to join, as a volunteer. It was widely regarded that the only way anyone could leave the IRA, was in a wooden box. That proved to be right in his case.

Billy clearly remembered too, the day after 'Bloody Sunday' as his whole school said prayers in the college chapel, for the victims. He felt at odds with everyone else. All he heard was how the Paras did this and the Paras did that, but this was his British army they were accusing of all these crimes and he felt like he shouldn't be there. He reasoned that if he had been a 19year-old 'Para' and the IRA started shooting at him and his mates, he would have started shooting back too, as you wouldn't know who was just an innocent bystander and who was a terrorist gunman, about to kill you. Anyway, why didn't his school ever say prayers for dead young British soldiers too? At that time, he realised, he had to put up with another 3 years in a school that was politically and religiously at odds with who he was and everything that he stood for! No wonder his qualifications were shit at the end of it all.

There was obviously a wide diversity of religious and political traditions in Billy's large family. Another of his cousins Brian, was in the British army and had to stay at Billy's for a week on one occasion, so that his dad could visit him. Billy's uncle Pat was an old WW2 hero and his nickname was 'Pat the Brit' He lived in Nationalist Andersonstown and was told by the Provisional IRA that as he was an old soldier, he wasn't a threat, but his son was regarded as a legitimate target, if he ever set foot on their patch. So, Billy's home in Loyalist Rathcoole became a safe house and his uncle visited Brian every day, before Brian went back to his regiment in West Germany.

During the height of the troubles in the mid-1970s, the office in which Billy worked, was evacuated at least once a week for bomb scares. Belfast was a war zone and so it became an integral part of the working lifestyle, to expect these incidents. It was rare that these were actual bombs, but unfortunately the IRA used the chaos of fear as a weapon in their campaign against the establishment. Billy's office in Windsor House in Bedford Street was particularly vulnerable, as the fire exits lead to a staircase beside plate glass windows. They often shattered when bombs went off and caused mostly cuts and abrasions to escaping workers. On more than few occasions, Billy had to walk the 5 miles home from Belfast, along with many other office workers, as the bus and transport system used to get so badly disrupted by the bomb scares.

Chapter 9:

Daily life in the 'Coole'

When Billy was little, his home estate of Rathcoole was a mixture of Protestant and Catholic families. As the troubles kicked off in the late 60s, quite a few nationalist minded Catholic families moved out. By about 1973, the provisional IRA had incurred such fear and hated among the Protestant population, that Catholics were all viewed as suspected Republican supporters. By 1974, almost all the Catholics had been petrol bombed out of their houses or had chosen to leave, voluntarily. The local commanders of the UDA discussed this situation. The father of One of Billy's friends was on the committee and vouched for Billy's family, as unionists, despite the fact, that they all had attended Catholic schools. He basically said 'leave the McCree family alone, they are okay!' Billy's family didn't know this at the time and they lived in fear of being petrol bombed out of their home, so every night for about a year, Billy's wooden Subbuteo table soccer board was placed against the back of the venetian blind in the living room, in the hope that any missile coming through the window would bounce back into the garden.

One night in the 1980s, Billy's friend Eric, who he had played in several bands with, asked him to go to the local working men's club. Apparently one of the guys from the local unemployed musicians club, had just got himself elected to the Newtownabbey town council. They had a party night, with 'Yard of Ale' drinking, games and raffles. At the end of the night about twenty of the party decided to go back to the musicians' club, above the shops in Rathcoole centre. They all arrived very noisily, with beer and cider etc, but no one had the key to the building. Obviously, one of the local residents rang the police, due to the late-night noise. A single police car pulled up in front of the crowd, at which point a couple of idiots immediately started throwing beer bottles at the car, shouting 'SS RUC!' An officer had just got out of the car, quickly weighed up the scenario and decided to call for back up. The police drove off to shouts of abuse and more bottles being thrown. Nearly 5 minutes later the drunken party were still unable to get into the building. Suddenly three large grey paddy wagons, came hurtling into the estate. About a dozen police got out and they meant to kick the shit out of the revellers for throwing bottles at their colleagues.

The drunken crowd panicked and scattered. Billy ran towards home, but he found that the police were now employing searchlights from the tops of the wagons, in a determined effort to locate anyone hiding in the dark from them. They picked up about 8 people and they were all charged with public affray and criminal damage, after getting a bloody good hiding with batons, inside the wagons. Billy had to lie in a garden for about 10 minutes, waiting for the searchlights to pass. He eventually got home, scared and cold and covered in mud from lying under a very wet hedge. He also realised his left hand had picked up some dog-pooh, as an extra souvenir of his escape from the police. Yuk!

On one other occasion Eric called with his brother-in-law Terry, to go for a drink in the Fern Lodge Pub. Billy hated the place, but Eric and Terry were both UVF members and the bar was owned by their friends. He thought to himself 'Yep, safe as houses!' After about 4 pints and a lot of catching up chat, they decided to leave. The toilet was on the way out and so they all popped in for a quick pee. Billy finished first and was shaking the water off his freshly washed hands, as he walked out the toilet door. He glanced up and saw that in the darkened hallway there stood a hooded gunman, with a large rifle pointing straight at him. He had a sudden weird thought that he could even see the tip of a bullet down the barrel. Eric and his brother-in-law wandered out of the toilet and immediately they were all ordered by a calm but threatening voice to lie down on the floor. Eric started to speak to the gunman and stuttered 'Are you IRA or what?' Billy was panicking like crazy inside and took advantage of this distraction. He pushed the rifle butt aside and fled out the door. The gunman could have shot him in the back, but luckily, he chose to concentrate on seeking out his prospective target in the main bar. As Billy ran across the car park, he spotted a car with blackened windows at the gate of the Pub and quickly realised this was probably the getaway car. He sprinted across the road behind the car and ran right around neighbouring Rushpark estate, on the other side of the Doagh Road. He chose to climb over some gates and through several back yards, in case he was somehow being followed. By the time he got to the opposite entrance of the estate, he felt it was safe to look back at the pub, which was now several hundred yards away. He noticed that the army had just arrived in the form of 3 armoured pigs. Billy impulsively ran back across the road towards them, but he suddenly realised that about four of them were pointing SLRs at him, as they had no idea who this maniac was running towards them. He put his hands up, as he ran shouting loudly, 'My friends are in there, did you catch the gunman?' The Sergeant ordered his men to lower their weapons and then engaged in questioning Billy about the whole incident. It transpired that the gunman had not been able to locate his intended prey and shot one round off into the roof of the Lounge bar, to ensure that he wasn't followed, as he escaped. The sinister car had gone too. After a while an unmarked police car pulled up. The plain clothes officer who got out, spoke to the army sergeant briefly and then approached Billy. He asked him to get into the car and he said would interview him as a witness, at the local station. Billy was then driven by the CID to the Whiteabbey station and once there, he had to describe the gunman and his driver in as much detail, as possible. He was asked what type of gun the gunman carried. Billy replied 'A big one!' He wasn't trying to be facetious, but in Northern Ireland everyone was assumed to be a weapons expert and Billy really didn't have a notion about one gun from another. He just knew they killed people! He was released after making a statement and after calming down with a large brandy at home, he called at Eric's house. Apparently, he and his brother-in-law both had to lie down on the floor of the bar foyer, while the gunman looked for his target. Eric reckoned that Billy had been mad for running out. 'He could have easily shot you in the back, you dick! You are either incredibly brave or just plain nuts! said Eric, as he shook his head. Ironically, the local news bulletin on the telly, gave a totally different description of both the gunman and his driver, from that given by Billy.

What was all that about and why did they even bother to interview him in the first place?

What was noticeable in Northern Ireland from the mid-70s, right through the troubles was the extremely low rate of petty or conventional crime. The Protestant paramilitaries ruled their own areas across the province and equally the Provisional IRA controlled all the Nationalist areas. The Police (Royal Ulster Constabulary) had to secretly agree times with the UDA, when they could patrol Rathcoole and it was rumoured that some police officers had professionally compromised their loyalties and were secretly members of the UDA or the UVF. This was one of the reasons why the Republicans wanted the RUC disbanded. They claimed it wasn't a fair or impartial Police force and only represented the rights of the Protestant population. It was alleged that some active Republicans had been shot and killed by the Protestant Paramilitaries on a number of occasions, due to illegal access of information from Police records. Maybe they had a point?

In Rathcoole, if a young delinquent or a gang decided to steal something like a bike or a set of golf clubs from an old man's garden shed or to mug an old lady coming from the shops, they needed to hope that the police caught them before the paramilitaries. Often on Saturday nights in the mid-70s, Billy would often be lying in his bed and he could hear the distant sound of .22 bullets, as petty criminals were shot through the knees, for their crimes. They were always shot in volleys of two... Bang, Bang! The culprits would be taken behind the burned out ruins of the old Alpha cinema building and a .22 Browning revolver placed behind the knee. These were known as punishment shootings and the republican areas governed themselves with similar tactics; only they used the more sinister tar and feathering too; for anyone who fraternised with the Army or the Police. Some of the lucky ones managed to get a prosthetic knee replacement and could walk again, albeit with a permanent limp, but a lot of these delinquents ended up in wheelchairs at just 16 or 17 years old. Consequently, by the late 1970s, Petty crimes just did not happen, not only in Rathcoole, but in most of the Housing Executive estates throughout Northern Ireland. The police were secretly glad, but they could not ever openly condone the Paramilitaries methods. It meant that they could get on with trying to fight the terrorists.

Billy's dad, Alan had his car broken into three times in two weeks. He parked the car on the grass in front of the house, instead of the usual car parking area at the ends of the street. A few nights later, Billy was woken at about 3am, by the sound of the car engine being revved. He jumped up shouting to his dad, 'Someone's nicking the car dad!' He pursued the thief down the street and quickly realised that the homemade lock and chain only allowed the car to turn left. The thief bounced the car off two kerbs and then a third one on the main road as the car ploughed into a ditch. He leapt out and run off into the night, as Billy reached the abandoned car. Immediately after, he heard an english accent shouting at him, to put his hands up. Billy looked up and saw six soldiers with SLR rifles pointed at him. 'It's my dad's car guys! I am in my pyjamas and slippers! Who steals a car in their jammies?' Alan arrived, out of breath. He shouted to the soldiers 'This is my car and my son!' After some intense explaining the soldiers helped them rescue the car and luckily the insurance covered the cost of repairs to the transmission and steering. A week later and Billy was with his friend Mark in a bar in the centre of Belfast. He spotted the car thief across the bar with three of his friends. He explained to Mark and he stood up laughing. 'Come with me!' he said, 'Let's have some fun!' Billy and Mark pushed in between their target and his startled friends. They were both wearing Crombie coats and looked very threatening. Billy smiled into the young man's face and said 'Hello! You don't know me, but I know that you stole my dad's yellow estate car last week and not for the first time! My friend here is the son of the Rathcoole UDA commander Stephen McGordon and he wants to rip your head off right now. I am a much nicer guy, however and I want to make you an offer. He will not tell his dad and have you knee-capped for car theft, so long as you never go near my dad's car again, nor set foot in my street. Basically, if we ever see your face again, in our part of the estate, you will regret it!' Without a word all four of the young men immediately jumped up and run out of the pub, as if a nuclear bomb had just gone off, leaving half-drunk pints. After a few seconds Billy turned to Mark and said 'Thank you mate, that felt fantastic. Just the look on your face scared the shit out of me! Neither of them ever set eyes on the thief again. There was even an unsubstantiated rumour that the troubled youth had been found dead in an alleyway a year later, from a drugs overdose.

Billy's friends called at his house one night, in Mark's car. Come on shouted Mark, we are all going to the Ian Paisley Rally in Belfast City Centre. It seems Mr. Paisley was complaining about the latest concessions that a frightened British government were making to the IRA, without considering the Loyalist position. There were over 200,000 people crowded around Belfast City Hall that night. The point was very solidly made to the British Government, about how they neglected the opinions and rights of the loyalist population, in appeasing the IRA and Sinn Fein with constant political concessions. These were plainly to stop them blowing Belfast City centre to hell.

No one paid much attention to the young lads collecting money in buckets for this worthy political cause, as they casually dropped cash into them on the way past. Some even had Ulster flags painted on the buckets. The next day the Belfast Telegraph newspaper reported that they had been Irish Nationalists in disguise. They sang orange songs, as they walked among the crowd; they exuded confidence and were just so plausible. They very definitely had balls and embarrassingly, ended up with about £25,000 of loyalist money too, by the end of that night! Totally embarrassing for the Unionists.

Billy had a girlfriend Sarah, from the Cliftonville Road, for a brief period in 1983. He had met her at an Inland Revenue staff do. She worked for Collection branch and he of course, worked for HM Tax Inspector. Sarah was very tall and skinny and always wore stockings and suspenders. Billy had never met a girl so outwardly sexy. To Billy most female Civil Service staff were conservative dressers in those days and if a boy mentioned sex, he was instantly regarded as a pervert! Sarah was a breath of fresh air to him. She had a best friend, Mary, who had a policeman for a boyfriend. Mary had had a history of Policemen boyfriends. Maybe she just liked the uniforms? Billy got to meet quite a few RUC men socially during this time and saw for himself some of the stresses and pressure they were under. They were all permanently armed and were regarded as primary targets, along with the army, by the provisional IRA. Many slept with their guns under their pillows at home and unfortunately a large number committed suicide, due to the demands and inherent dangers of the job, or else they were blown up by IRA bombs planted under their cars. Billy had wanted to be a policeman once, when he was a teenager, but soon decided that although he greatly admired them, he could never handle the pressure of the job himself. One night, Billy and Sarah went out as a foursome with Mary and her policeman. They accidentally drove into a riot near Tigers Bay, off Belfast's York Road. Suddenly, Mark unholstered his handgun and held it down towards the floor or Billy's dad's car. He was terrified, in case the car was stopped by the rioters, as Mark would certainly have used the gun on any potential attackers. He also thought that his Dad would kill him, if anything happened to the car. They somehow negotiated the angry crowd with just a few stones bouncing off the car and Billy managed to squeeze past a few burning petrol bombs on the ground, without damage to his Dad's Cortina estate. Later that evening, after a few drinks to calm them down; they all went back to the Police station, where Mark 'lived in'. The station had a small section house, where about a third of the officers lived.

Suddenly Billy and Sarah found themselves alone, as Mark had decided to give Mary a guided tour of the station. Billy had been away for most of the previous week at a Trade Union Conference and so Sarah had missed his attentions. Both were feeling the urgent need for physical bliss and they made the most of the time alone on top of Mark's bed. They had just finished having a 'quickie', when the irate station Duty Sergeant knocked the door, demanding they leave right away. They both stared innocently at the sergeant, as they walked towards the station door. Sarah was apologising to the Sergeant, but claimed they had simply been sitting on the bed, waiting for their friends return. Mark was reminded loudly and abruptly that servicing officers were not permitted to leave friends unattended in their accommodation. He was told he would be on a charge, if it happened again! Phew...they had nearly got caught in the act. What a strange and unusual place to have sex? It certainly was one for Billy to boast about, over a pint with his mates, at some later date.

Billy used to visit Sarah at her home regularly, during the week. Her dad was always out, as he worked late and her mum was recovering from a knee operation and could not leave the living room, without help. They used to have some great heavy petting sessions in her large front lounge, as they knew they wouldn't be interrupted. One night, they had been having a lovely time and suddenly both realised it had got very late. Sarah's mum interrupted them, just as Billy had orgasmed. She needed Sarah to help her to the toilet and Billy's taxi had arrived at the same time he had! On hearing her mum's voice, he instantly pulled up and zipped up his trousers. He was wishing he had brought his dad's car as he got into the cab, still wearing a 'full' condom. The taxi driver asked him if he had had a good night. Billy felt secretly embarrassed at his situation and for once didn't make small talk with the driver. He just replied 'yes' and then only spoke again to ask the amount of his fare. It had been an uncomfortable journey home, but he was relieved to eventually get to his own bathroom and clean himself up.

The following week, he brought the car and left Sarah's house at just after 2:30am. He reached the roundabout at Cliftonville Circus and slowed almost to a stop, but not quite. Glancing down the Cliftonville Road, he spotted another car heading towards him, but realised it was a safe enough distance from him and proceeded to drive across the roundabout. Suddenly a Police 'Paddy Wagon' came out of nowhere. He was flashed at, pulled up and surrounded by six RUC men with machine guns. It was a disgraceful and threatening show of power to a lone driver, in the middle of the night. He was breathalysed, which was negative, of course. He was intensely questioned, as the car was his father's and not his. He had to stand like a naughty schoolboy, while a female PC, still in the wagon, took his details and charged him with reckless driving. The car had been MOT'd a few weeks before, but they walked around it like strutting Nazis in a Warsaw ghetto, checking every light and every brake and tyre. It was quite an ordeal and Billy was shaking like a leaf. He had always wondered why the Catholics hated the Police so much. The way he was treated that night made him realise! They really were a vindictive paramilitary style force! It seemed like any encounter with the RUC was like meeting the Gestapo in those days. Billy appeared in court a few weeks later and took his fine on the chin. Luckily, he had met a solicitor before the hearing, who could not believe that Billy didn't have one. (He couldn't afford a Solicitor). He was advised not to naively plead 'Not Guilty', as his word against the Police would not hold up in court. The friendly Solicitor told him he must admit guilt and say sorry to the Careless Driving charge, then tell the judge that it would never happen again. Billy received a written endorsement on his licence and a £50 fine. Using Sarah's friend's contacts on the force, he found out that the Police who stopped him were all from nearby Oldpark barracks and they had been trying to boost the arrest record of the 'Rookie' female PC, who was just out of Enniskillen training college. Billy had been their unfortunate prey. He was the victim of aggressive over-policing and had just been in the wrong place at the wrong time.

The relationship with Sarah didn't last, as She was a very fickle and free spirit and she made it very plain that she didn't want anything serious in her life, at that time. Ironically, Billy was madly in love and it really broke his heart when she dropped him. He had been more than a bit naïve about how relationships worked at that point and had perhaps not given her her space at times, when she needed it. He basically tried to suffocate her with his love, with the obvious result!

Rathcoole estate was governed by the paramilitaries. Anything that happened there had to be endorsed by the UDA and occasionally by the UVF. The biggest problem was that the larger predominant UDA, with their military wing the UFF, were often at loggerheads with the older and more established UVF. As Loyalists they were all meant to be on the same side, or so it appeared? Except that sometimes their differences boiled over into a gang war and the real enemy, the IRA would mockingly accuse them of murdering each other, instead of concentrating on the fight with them. Somehow, they kept the lid on this insane rivalry and the local population felt reasonably safe, most of the time, from attack by Republican fanatics. The army occasionally raided houses in Rathcoole, due to tip offs about illegal weapons hoarding by these paramilitaries, but strangely Rathcoole was one of the safer places to live in Northern Ireland during the troubles.

When it came to social activities, there was only the Alpha club, (run by the UDA) or the Cool Social Club on O'Neill road, at the top of the estate, (run by the UVF), as local places to drink. The Fern Lodge Pub, on the Doagh Road, was a possible third venue, but it had a seriously scary reputation for fights and stabbings. Billy drank in the Alpha because of his friendship with the son of a UDA commander. This fact alone made him feel safe, However, one Sunday night Billy and his friend Sam, were having a quiet beer, but were given a lot of verbal abuse by a local thug, called 'Turk' and his equally scary friend Mad Eddie.

Turk had first met Billy when he was 16, in the Cloughfern Arms, which was a over a mile away and belonged to the adjacent estate of Rathfern. In those days, nobody bothered much about ID and proof of age in out-of-town Bars. If you looked 18, then no questions were asked.

Billy's next-door neighbour, Geordie, knew Turk from school and they all happened to be in the Cloughfern Arms at the same time. There were a lot of underage drinkers in the pub that night and when Billy and Geordie were walking home, a little worse for wear, Turk and Mad Eddie ambushed them and basically gave them a kicking. Billy had lost a large tuft of his long wavy hair, in the fight, but managed to break free and run home. He was covered in blood from a gash on the head and his earlobe was hanging on by a tiny bit of skin, but he was otherwise okay. It seems that Turk wanted Geordie, because of an old grudge in school from years earlier and Billy just got in the way.

Since that night, all those years before, Turk had found out more about Billy's mixed religious background and now he really wanted an excuse to give him another kicking. In Turk's eyes Billy was just a dirty Fenian. Except for those two occasions, he didn't actually know him at all. Billy had always managed to avoid this known 'Psychotic' kid, around the estate. On that particular Sunday night, Turk and his friend were eventually persuaded to leave by the bouncers, who noticed their raised voices and threatening behaviour to someone else, on a nearby table. Everyone in the bar could see they were trouble waiting to happen. Shortly after they left, a regular member of the club came across and asked Billy 'Was he giving you a hard time, by any chance?' 'Ah…no it's okay' replied a startled Billy. The enquirer then leaned a little closer and said 'Seriously son, I can get that bastard done if you want. He's a cunt anyway and a there are a lot of people who would love to see him dead! We don't allow anyone to pick fights in this club or harass our friends!' Billy smiled nervously, felt himself getting butterflies of pure terror in his stomach and answered 'No thank you, really. I am not into that sort of thing, but I thank you for your kind offer of help!'

When they got outside, Sam said 'That guy meant that you know, plenty of people want Turk dead.' Billy gulped and muttered 'I know that, that's why I nearly shit a brick! I am not a gangster and I would not want to think that I was even indirectly responsible for anyone's death, not even that evil shitbag!'

The paramilitaries always looked after their friends, but their modus operandi was like the 'Cosa Nostra' and enemies were shown no mercy! If Billy had taken up the offer of having Turk killed, he would have then been obliged to do a series of favours in return, such as perhaps hiding illegal weapons in his loft, or perhaps having to assist in a punishment shooting on someone, himself. But, being a man of some integrity, he managed to stay clear of any involvement in such sensitive paramilitary matters.

Chapter 10:

Holiday Memories

When he was little, Billy remembered his dad taking the family to Millisle and Cloughey in the beautiful Ards Peninsula, for day trips to the beach. These were great times, but they were only single days out, as Alan couldn't afford to take the family away anywhere for a full weeks' holiday. The beaches were lovely and often quiet and uncluttered. They were perfect for a young family. Both Millisle and Cloughey had just a corner beach shop for supplies and a basic public toilet, so it usually meant that the family had to drive back up to the larger towns of Donaghadee or Bangor if they wanted to shop or get things like fish and chips. It was always a fun day out for the family, even though the car was full and no one wore seatbelts back then. Granny Cameron used to occasionally pay for family day trips to Newcastle in Co. Down or to Omeath, which was across the Irish border, as a special treat. In those days every car was searched and you had to show passports or other appropriate ID at the border. Northern drivers had to apply in advance for a green triangular sticker/permit to show on their windscreen too. Omeath was a lovely little market village, from where visits to nearby King John's castle at Carlingford, were a must. Billy remembered one occasion when his dad's car had a handbrake problem. Alan was in the Southern Irish border office and his large Vauxhall Wyvern started to roll back down the slight gradient. Quickly, Billy and his brother and sister jumped out of the car and started frantically trying to push it back up the road. Jeanette and granny Cameron, who had Agnes on her knee, were still in the car. It must have looked bizarre as the Customs officer looked out the window at the three shrieking kids trying in vain, to push this huge car back up the hill. The bewildered, worried smiles emanating from mum and granny in the car, must have made it look even more bizarre. Alan didn't bat an eyelid and calmly picked up his legal papers. He gently jogged back to the car. It was picking up speed as he jumped in and he simply put his foot on the brake to stop it and at the same time slid the car in second gear without the engine running. Billy and his terrified siblings got back into the car. Alan was laughing at their anxiety and chirped 'It's okay you lot, I'll just get it fixed next week in the garage! I'll just have to park up somewhere flat for the rest of the day.' Heading back home later, Alan parked on a much more level part of the road, before going into the customs office and thankfully there was no repeat of the rolling episode from earlier. Just in case, Billy sat in the driver's seat with his foot on the brake, until Alan returned from the Customs office.

In later years, they had caravan holidays in a little caravan park called Coney Island, near the fishing port of Ardglass. It was tiny and absolutely nothing like its namesake in New York. The family would have days out in Ardglass, Killough and also Downpatrick, which often included a trip on the Portaferry ferry boat. This was usually the highlight of these holidays. Life was so simple back then, in the days before package holidays to Greece and Spain. One year, Alan took them all to Ballycastle's Moyle View caravan Park and apart from getting hammered by his sister Anne at tennis every day, Billy chased a pretty brunette at the small amusement park. He thought he was getting on well with this girl until a much bigger local lad and two of his friends had him against the wall outside the chip shop and told Billy, he would get his throat ripped out if he was seen near the girl again. She obviously belonged to one of the local lads. Billy stuck to eating 'Yellow man' candy and dulce (seaweed) for the rest of the week, and getting battered at Tennis by his much more skilful sibling.

His regular friends were Mark, Sam, Ricky, Stan and Paul. From the age of 18 Paul was almost always away with the Royal Navy, but in the summer of 1982, they all decided to go to Ibiza for a two week 'lads' holiday. Mark was always the richest and smartest, so he was the unofficial group leader. Billy was the oldest and most sensible (most of the time) and Sam was the quiet, slightly boring one. Ricky was just mischievous and daft and usually brought out the worst in the rest of the group. Stan was the drunk and Paul was the fighter. The chemistry between them was often fun, but it could be volatile too. It meant that this holiday was going to be interesting.

Billy and Mark walked the 4 kilometres into San Antonio on the first night, to see a solo artist doing Don McLean and Simon and Garfunkel songs, in a very noisy live music bar 'La Pacha'. The venue had quite a few forty ounce bottles of Bacardi and Gin lined up on a rack above the bar. The pair couldn't find a seat and so they stood at the bar cradling their drinks. Suddenly, Mark dared Billy to try to nick one of the large full spirit bottles, above his head. Billy was only wearing a teeshirt, but after assessing the logistics, he realised loads of other people in the bar had their shirts off, in the hot evening air. Within a moment, his shirt was off and the busy bar staff didn't notice him swiftly grab a Bacardi bottle, from the top of the bar and hide it as discreetly as possible, wrapped in his tee-shirt. Needless to say they both made a very quick exit from the bar. If they had been caught of course, the Spanish police would have surely dealt with them severely. It was a foolish thing to do, but they thought it was exciting!

On the plane journey there, the whole group had decided on a challenge to see who could have sex with a girl first. Mark thought he was being sneaky by deciding to find a brothel for him and Billy that night. It was about 3am, but he was determined to get them both a woman. They went to a little back street brothel in San Antonio. The whole affair cost them 7000 pesetas each (just over £50 back then) and poor Billy was just so drunk, he couldn't manage to do the business. The girl he had been given was a true Spanish beauty, with beautiful long black hair and she was ready to do practically anything for him. The girls' minders were scary and looked like the traffickers from the movie 'Taken', so there would be no argument about paying. The next morning over breakfast, Mark and Billy announced to the gang what they had done. The rest of the lads got angry and complained that Mark and Billy had broken the rules by paying for it and so they were immediately disqualified from the game. Billy was full of remorse, especially as he had spent about a third of his holiday budget, in one night and he was now thinking about visiting the GUM clinic on his return to Belfast. He needed to be careful about his spending for the rest of his holiday. He had to give up his bed on another night for Ricky, to accommodate a young lady friend from Leeds. The lads had been sharing 3 to a room and so Stan was turfed out of the room too. That night Billy and Stan slept very uncomfortably, on the sunbeds by the pool. The stars looked lovely at about 3 am! 'Anything to help a horny mate get his corn!' he thought, as they shivered while watching the sun come up. Billy didn't realise that Spain got so cold at night, especially in July. It was not much warmer than home!'

The next afternoon, Sam asked could he borrow Billy's guitar. He was trying to sunbathe and so he just agreed to let him have it. A little while later, Billy was lying on his sunbed and thought 'Hang on a minute, my guitar is left-handed and Sam is right handed! What the hell is going on?' Feeling very curious, Billy went off around the hotel grounds, looking for Sam. He soon found him and Ricky standing outside the chalet of two beautiful Swedish sisters, trying their best to serenade them. They both had sombreros and guitars and Ricky even had a flower in his mouth. Billy was laughing to himself, but kept his distance, to see how they got on. Within a minute of them starting to sing, a massive, muscle bound, Swedish bloke (obviously the father) came out of the sliding doors on the front of the chalet and started swearing and shaking his fists at them both. They nearly shit and even dropped one of the sombreros as they sprinted to safety. Billy who was not noticed at all by the Swedish gentleman, was pissing himself laughing, as he watched them disappear in terror. He picked up the abandoned sombrero and put it on, as he strolled back to the room to empathise and commiserate with his distressed friends.

The following day two pretty English girls arrived at the hotel from Shropshire. Billy fancied one of them, who he called 'Clodagh', as she was the spitting double of the Newry born singer, Clodagh Rogers. It became obvious after a couple of days that neither of the girls fancied any of the group, but they knew that Irish lads were good fun and so hung around with them for the rest of the holiday, just as friends. 'Clodagh' picked up the paper one morning and read about the notorious 'Hyde Park' bombing, an evil act carried out by the IRA on unsuspecting guardsmen and their horses. Immediately the two sisters got extremely angry with Billy and his mates, just for being Irish. Sam indignantly followed them and took them both aside. He explained that he and his friends were all loyalists and British and that not only did they not condone the bombing, but they were all actively campaigning or fighting at home, against the IRA. It was suddenly plain to Billy and his friends that most English people at that time, had little clue about what was really going on in Northern Ireland. The girls were fine with them all after this and even felt enlightened about the politics involved. They were also quite sympathetic too, when they thought about the stranglehold that the Troubles had on the boys' lifestyles.

Sam and Stan then tried to teach Clodagh and her sister how to speak in a Belfast accent. It was hilarious. The chosen phrase (written colloquially) was 'Yew an' me on a pigs back muckar, we'll be alected!' In plain English it means 'We are good friends and can go anywhere and do anything together!' The Shropshire accents were so posh to Billy and his friends, that they just laughed hilariously at their attempts to speak 'Belfast'.

The rest of the holidaymakers around the pool, just thought they were all nuts.

That evening, Billy got to sing in a holiday talent show, in the hotel ballroom. The prizes were all bottles of alcohol, as Spanish employment laws forbade cash prizes. He was doing very well, singing Neil Diamond and Beatles covers and he signalled the lads to get up to dance, as he finished his short set with a version of the Conga on the acoustic guitar. Ricky and Paul mischievously decided to lead about 40 hotel guests in the conga line down the steps to the pool, which had just been cleaned, ready for the next morning. As soon as the song finished, they all jumped into the pool fully clothed. Next morning, Billy was woken by Mark with a letter, in English, from the hotel management banning all of them from the pool for two days, with a warning they would all have to leave the hotel, if they couldn't refrain from this irresponsible behaviour. The pool stunt definitely had not gone down well. That day Billy and Ricky took guitars to the beach and entertained a very crowded Playa d'en Bossa, with their versions of Hotel California and the Shadows 'Summer Holiday, among others. They felt like rock stars for the day and did get a lot of promising attention from young ladies on the beach. The rest of the holiday was drunken fun, but it was fairly uneventful, compared to what had gone before and the Hotel didn't have to throw them out in the end.

The following summer, the boys decided to go to Blackpool for a week instead of abroad, as money was a bit tight for a few of them. Sam and Ricky had had the expense of buying cars, earlier on in the year. Paul couldn't go, as he was actually stationed in Hong Kong with the Navy.

There was only one sunny day in that whole week's holiday. Billy decided it would be cool to wear just an open waistcoat, instead of a shirt, for some bizarre reason. At the end of the day, he looked like an Ajax footballer, with a huge stripe of 'red' in the middle of his chest from the sun and pure white shoulders and ribcage. That got some laughs from the lads later!

On another afternoon, the group met some lads from Glasgow and got friendly with them over a few beers, in Coral Island. They had been chatting about the best places in Blackpool to meet girls and so decided to go to the huge, Tiffany's night club that evening. No one knew where Tiffany's was in relation to the Hotel and in those days, there were no mobile phones to 'google' it. The boys smugly booked two taxis for 10 people and were literally taken round the corner and about fifty metres along the next road. There it was, Tiffany's Night Club. The taxis cost two pound each (which was a fair amount in 1983) and they felt like daft buggers, when the walk would have been no more than two minutes. Some bewildered glances appeared between them, followed by some embarrassed laughter. Neither taxi driver batted an eyelid, when it would have been obvious to call them all lazy gits, or simply point out their lack of local geographical knowledge! Still, a fare is a fare!

In the club, Billy met a girl he knew, called Paula from the Belfast Tax office. She had the hots for him, but he just didn't fancy her. She kept being a nuisance and wouldn't leave Billy alone, so he left Tiffany's with his mate Stan, after just a short period of time. The two of them went to see the Black Abbott's comedy show at the North Pier instead of dancing the night away. The next day Sam turned up with Paula on his arm. It was obvious that there was a chemistry between them and so Billy had to get used to her being around. The rest of the holiday was just boozing and trying to keep Stan out of fights. Sure enough, Stan had a fight with three of the Glasgow lads, as they mistakenly took something he said while drunk, as being an IRA supporter. After breaking up the fight in the Hotel, with only a few bruises all round, Mark calmly explained that it had been a total misunderstanding and showed the Scots lads his Rangers supporters membership card. We are all prods here lads. You know 'Unionists, British, yeah!!' In Stan's case, it was a case of, you can take the drunken gobshite out of Belfast, but you can't take Belfast out of the drunken gobshite!

The following year Mark had an idea to go off backpacking in the Greek Islands. He had some fantastic brochures from the travel agent and Billy thought Greece looked amazing. He kept talking about the Cyclades group of islands and doing some island hopping. Most of the lads had either already booked holidays with girlfriends or family or were working on the dates when Mark wanted to go. Billy had to borrow several days from his next year 'Annual Leave' allowance in work, but he managed somehow to get the time off work to go. So, Mark and Billy got the train to Dublin on a wet Sunday morning in August 1984. They went from there to Dublin Airport and had to spend a whole day there, as their flight to Athens was at the strange time of

3:20am the next morning. There was a two-hour time difference and so it was mid-morning local time, when they arrived in Athens airport. He noticed straight away that there was a very Middle Eastern feel about the airport.

Billy had never seen a Muslim before, as there were very few in Northern Ireland in the 1980s. He was fascinated by the clothes, hijabs, turbins and the prayer mats that were evident all around the arrivals lounge and he soon realised that Athens was and of course still is a significant gateway to the East. Billy thought, 'this is certainly very different from Spain'. He wondered if Greece was a Muslim country. Up until then he had never been to any other country but Spain, but by the time the Airport coach arrived in the centre of Athens, he could clearly see that Greece had a mainly Christian European/ Mediterranean identity and that the scenes at the airport were just another part of this Cosmopolitan City. They agreed to stay for only a couple of nights in Athens, mainly to allow them time to visit the famous Parthenon, Acropolis and flea markets. After wandering around exploring Athens all day, Billy was very tired and in need of his hotel bed. They both sampled local Moussaka in a restaurant in Syntagma Square and went straight back to their room to sleep. Mark was restless however, and he woke up very noisily at 3am. He coyly asked could he borrow some Drachmas from Billy. They had only been allowed to bring a limited amount of Drachmas into the country and had arranged to cash some travellers' cheques, the next day. Billy asked why Mark had so urgently wakened him in the middle of the night. He wanted a woman, as it turned out. Billy was completely exhausted and he just didn't want to go out, so he gave

Mark the cash to pay for his light entertainment. Just over two and a half hours later Mark came back knackered, but with a happy grin. He had had his wicked way with two young ladies and spent all their cash. It had been a foolish thing to do, alone in the red-light area of a City he didn't know, as he could have been mugged, robbed or beaten up and Billy would have had to cope on his own, if anything terrible had happened. Billy was pleased that Mark had had a nice time, but he reminded him of the dangers of his impulsive behaviour, before they both went back to sleep.

The rest of their short visit was just that of typical tourists and in accordance with their planned itinerary they arrived at Piraeus harbour two days later. They embarked on a large ship for the beautiful island of Ios. Billy thought how large this ship was compared to his regular trips on the Belfast/Liverpool ferry. It was an overnight journey and they spent most of the time playing cards or sightseeing on deck. Onboard ship overnight, they drank about 36 cans of Lowenbrau. They stacked all the empty cans into a pyramid, in one corner of the lounge. The stewards thought they were nuts and one even playfully remarked 'You Irish…don't you do anything else but drink?' The ship stopped off at the islands of Paros and Naxos, during the night and was continuing on to Santorini, after Billy and Mark got off. It was a regular daily ferry service between the main islands in the 'Cyclades' group. On the island of Ios, they quickly found a campsite near the small port and hurriedly pitched their tent. That first night, Billy couldn't sleep because of something he had read in a book about dangerous scorpions in Greece. The next morning, he heard three familiar Northern Irish, male accents in the tent beside theirs. Billy started to chat to one of the occupants of the adjoining tent, while having a morning wash at the standing water tap. It turned out their neighbours were three lads from Lisburn and Billy immediately concluded they must be protestants. He started to verbally insult Irish nationalists, as he always did, but was met by an uncomfortable silence. He didn't get to speak to these lads again, until late that afternoon in the old-fashioned town centre.

Ios was a stunning place. It was very hilly and had little open-air Tavernas, cafes and beautiful small beaches teeming with optionally naked and semi-naked sunbathers. The smell of Souvlakis cooking on the charcoal grills along the beach Tavernas, was permanently in the air and because of this Billy felt permanently hungry. He noticed just how many crazy, beautiful and very naked foreign ladies there were on the beach and thought it was absolute paradise for any young man. He then spotted two well-endowed naked, French guys playing frisbees and quickly decided that he was not even going to try to compete. He would most definitely be keeping his swimming trunks on for the entire holiday and kept thinking 'Huh, who said size isn't everything!'

Mark and Billy met up with their campsite neighbours again that afternoon and started to chat properly over a beer. The lads were called Rob, Steve and Brian and all three worked in the Belfast shipyard. Rob was the bass player in a heavy rock outfit called 'Steel Ravage' from Belfast. They had toured with Thin Lizzy, as their warm-up act on a British tour, the previous year and were quite famous in Northern Ireland. Billy had seen them perform the previous year in the Pound Music Club, in Belfast and as a heavy metal fan himself, he really liked their music. Mark soon realised that a large percentage of the pretty girls on the island were in fact tourists like themselves and most were also students from Queens University in Belfast or from Trinity College in Dublin and they all knew Rob. He was a legend and a 'hottie' to most of them and so Billy and Mark decided they might just hang around with Rob and his friends, in case they might have a chance with any of Rob's rejected hareem. This became the start of a great twelve days on the island and another rogue campsite rocker from Bristol, became the sixth member of the group. After a second night in the campsite, they found a basic guesthouse at 1100 drachmas for 11 nights. It worked out about £9 each in total. This was madly cheap, even in the eighties, but all six of them were easily accommodated. It did have just a very basic shower and no bedding, so the boys all slept in their sleeping bags every night.

Rob turned out to be a catholic and it was 4 days before he told Billy, as he had taken from their initial exchanges that Billy was a loyalist extremist and he was more than a bit frightened to say anything. As they all got to know each other, they realised they were all heavily into Rock music and Billy explained to Rob about his mixed background and why he had such strong political views. Rob was not an Irish Nationalist, as it transpired, but he did still go to his local Catholic church on Sundays, when he was at home. He said it was mainly to please his mum. The issue was never discussed again.

They got to know some of the naked sunbathers on the beach. Some of these ladies were already Rob's friends or 'groupies' and Billy struck up a rapport with one pretty redhead called Linda. He thought he was doing well and arranged to have a quiet drink with her that night in the Village. She didn't turn up and Mark and Billy went to the Scorpions night club till 4am, instead. By the time they got back to the guesthouse, they were both very drunk and just jumped into their sleeping bags, as usual. They couldn't turn the light on, as they did not want to waken Rob, who was sharing with them and they both quickly went to sleep. Billy woke up first at around 8am. The room had heavy wooden shutters on the window, which meant it was in complete darkness, until they were opened up by hand on a morning. Billy decided to open the shutters and the first thing he saw was Rob lying with Linda's legs wrapped around him. This was a quite a shock and made Billy feel like an ugly reject. He also felt a little betrayed by Rob and very stupid, as he had until that point, naively thought he had a chance with Linda. Despite flirting whenever he could, Billy didn't get anywhere near another girl for the rest of the holiday. It strengthened his already held believe that he really was just an ugly skinny dude, with little to offer any girl!

The next night Billy got a sort of revenge on Rob. He didn't tell Rob that Mark was capable of some incredible drinking feats. He was a big lad and could consume large amounts of alcohol with very little effect. In the busy Taverna, Rob and Billy watched as Mark had consumed four large Tequilas, carefully observing the famous salt and lemon ritual. Rob had never seen this before and wanted to try it for himself. The Greek barmen never measured their alcohol and so Mark winked at the Barman, as he poured nearly a half pint of Tequila into a glass. Rob was already quite drunk from Lowenbrau, but drank the Tequila with the salt and lemon. Billy nudged Mark saying 'That measure was much larger than yours!' Mark laughed and replied 'Come on, we'll get the daft bugger another one!' Billy then proceeded to call Rob a wimp and a lightweight and egged him on to have another Tequila. He winked to the barman and the measure was even larger again. Rob drank it quickly in one and he had just managed to slide the empty glass back onto the bar. He looked extremely groggy at this point. Mark swiftly read the situation and anticipated his reaction. He stooped slightly behind Rob's bar stool and picked him up in a fireman's lift, as he almost simultaneously fell back. He was totally out cold from the alcohol!'

Mark politely excused himself, promising he would be back in a few minutes. He then casually carried Rob out of the Taverna on his shoulders, through the village and back to the guest house, where he dumped him unceremoniously on his bed. It was like something from a John Wayne movie. Rob slept right through till 2 pm the next day and he couldn't sunbathe, because of his hangover and the unbearable headache that came with it. He certainly wasn't going to be any use to Linda that night! There were many opportunities to play guitar and sing on that holiday, so Billy cursed himself for not bringing his guitar, due to the size and weight of his backpack. He saw it as a missed opportunity to improve his standing as a musician.

After the holiday, they all stayed friends and frequently met up in Belfast's Botanic Inn for drinks on Friday nights. The 'Bot' was the best student bar at the time. Billy was lead guitarist in one of his bands at this point and so he often arrived late, after rehearsals. He still used to try to pose alongside Rob and the other 'Steel Ravagers' at the bar, trying to look like some kind of a rock star and desperately hoping that the female student customers, also saw him as such. He deep down felt like an ugly amateur, but what the hell! It was fun to try to act out his dream.

As a joke, Mark had got Rob's mate Brian to burst in on Billy one night in the shower room while in their digs in Ios. He had taken a photo of him naked, in mid shower. Remember, where they stayed had been very basic accommodation and so the showers were always cold. It is understandable that Billy had an appropriately shrivelled manhood, on that occasion. He had completely forgotten about this photo until now, then Mark laughingly explained that it had just been passed around every corner of the pub and so not only was Billy the object of humour, but he was never likely to get a date with any of the female students again. Mark thought it was all very funny, but once again his wicked sense of humour had demeaned Billy. Billy thought 'Friends do the most hurtful things sometimes!' It took a while for the subsequent nickname 'Wee Billy' to wear off, as you can imagine!

Chapter 11:

Guns and Stuff

Billy's mate Stan had a brother, Greg. Greg was in the RUC reserve for a couple of years and then decided he wanted to change to the Ulster Defence Regiment (UDR). They were the local regiment of the Army reserve (TAVR) to start with. Gradually, as their numbers swelled, they took on more and more of the regular army duties. This allowed the regular Army to give more soldiers longer leave and eventually to use less full-time soldiers in the whole Northern Ireland set up. The UDR were the only regiment allowed to be armed 24/7. Greg came back from a shift one night and Stan had all the gang, including Billy, at home. They had been watching a Pink Floyd concert on the telly. Greg had been on duty for 14 hours and being very tired, left his SLR rifle standing up against the wall. The lads had been drinking and when Greg went to the kitchen to get something to eat, Mark picked up the rifle and pointed it at Stan. He was laughing and teasing 'I bet this would take your head off, if I shot you now!' He thought it was great fun. Greg nearly freaked when he came back in the room. 'Put the gun down carefully, right now Mark' he yelled. 'Don't fuck about or I will be on a serious charge!' Mark shrugged, realising he shouldn't have picked the gun up. He handed the rifle back to Greg, straight away, butt end first. Greg immediately put the safety catch back on the gun. Due to his tired state, he had forgotten to do this before. Greg quickly explained that the trigger is mega sensitive and that if he had so much as jerked his hand a little too hard, Mark would have made a tiny bullet hole in the front of Stan's head. The back of his head would probably have blown off completely and the bullet would have likely lodged somewhere in the back-yard wall, more than 30 feet away. This was the nature of a high velocity bullet. Everyone was stunned, at how close this came to happening and this was the nervous cue for them all to go home.

Billy saw Greg again one afternoon, sitting outside his front door. He looked really sad and down in the dumps. 'What's up mate? Are you okay?' he asked. 'No Billy, as a matter of fact I am not!' Greg proceeded to tell him the story about his best friend Simon. He had been best man at Simon's wedding the year before. Simon was a full-time RUC reservist. He had worked near Crossmaglen for months, on daily patrol in the famous 'Bandit territory' alongside the regular army. He had done about 5 or 6 stints of duty down there, before being transferred to permanent security duty at Castlereagh Police Station, in Belfast. Simon had become addicted to the adrenalin rush he got while working around the dangerous border area and so he found that opening and closing gates for vehicles at Castlereagh barracks, was an extremely tedious and boring existence, by comparison. He then went into a deep depression and like so many stressed policemen at the time, he was found dead in his car, one morning in a Belfast park. He was still holding his revolver in his hand, when they found him. Greg was devastated at the loss of his friend and was trying to get his head together to visit Simon's wife. As Billy walked away, feeling sad for his friend's loss, he was once again relieved that he had never followed up on his childhood desire to join the Police force. His love for the 1970s television series 'The Sweeney' almost had a lot to answer for!

Billy thought about two other friends who had worked with him in the Tax office. They used to all play together in the Revenue Offices Darts league on Thursday nights, in Hannigan's Bar in Fountain Street, near the City Centre. They had both left the daily tedium and routine of the Tax office for the apparent excitement and better wages of being in the security forces. One joined the RUC Police reserve and the other the UDR. Both were legally allowed to carry handguns 24/7, for their own protection, as they were now regarded as legitimate targets of the Provisional IRA. One night they joined the Tax office crowd in the upstairs lounge, for old times' sake. They just fitted in with their old office colleagues and the night was going well. The toilets were downstairs and so at one point, after a few beers, they were both heading down there together. Suddenly a lone, masked gunman appeared and opened fire from the bottom of the stairs. He shot up the stairs twice, but somehow missed his two targets and hit the wall. One bullet ricocheted and put a hole through the upstairs window. Their assailant sprinted off, as one of his potential victims shot two rounds off after him, in the street. He didn't want to shoot anymore, in case he accidentally hit a civilian bystander. Within minutes there were three armoured pigs full of soldiers and two police wagons in the street. Unfortunately, they never caught the terrorist gunman, who slipped quietly into what was a typical cold, wet night. He had obviously been an IRA volunteer and it was later concluded that someone in the pub had recognised the two men as RUC/Army and rang the local Provos to have them taken out. Luckily, no one was hurt, but Billy was told in no uncertain terms by his Tax office colleagues, never to bring his 'bodyguards' with him to any more darts matches.

No one in Belfast liked the body searches, as you came in and out of Belfast City centre during the Troubles. However, most people agreed that it was necessary to ensure a level of safety, for those working in the City Centre. There were barriers across every thoroughfare, with full time Civilian searchers, paid by the Northern Ireland Office of the Civil Service. Each entrance to the City Centre also had armed soldiers, in case anything ever kicked off or someone didn't want to be searched. Sometimes, if you were in the city centre late at night, the army would make you fill in forms with your address and details, before letting you leave the secure area. This meant they could monitor who had been in the City and up to what time, if late night bombs went off or any violence broke out. They randomly stopped and searched cars too, which was meant to deter drivers from entering the City. It was all part of a tight security set up, to combat the IRA bombing campaign and try to reassure the general public.

Billy took several friends for a day trip to Dublin, one summer's day. He hadn't had either the car or his full licence very long and so he relished the challenge of driving the 100 miles or so, each direction. There were 4 of them in the car, Billy, Sam, Stan and Stan's girlfriend. They stopped at a shopping mall near Drogheda, for refreshments and there was a record shop playing 'The Green Fields of

France'. None of them had heard the song before and didn't know the lyrics, or what it was about, so because of its' familiar folk style, they took it to be a rebel Irish song and all of them, feeling intimidated by it, ran back to the car. They didn't find out until weeks later, that it was actually a sad first world war tribute to a volunteer British soldier and was a big hit in the Irish charts for the Fureys.

When they got to Dublin, the first realisation was that it had no security barriers and it was entirely free to walk around the city. Sam observed this difference very jealously and Billy thought how ironic it was that Southern Ireland was safe from bombs, while his City was rampaged every week by Southern Irish fanatics. Stan particularly enjoyed the real 'Liffey water'...Guinness and they visited the famous Baggot Inn, where Thin Lizzy and Brush Shiels used to jam.

Stan wanted to visit St. Mitchan's church in Dublin, which had the original lectern that Handel used for his music, when he first performed the 'Messiah' in 1742. The Norman knight Strongbow had bizarrely stored his heart in a metal ball case, on one of the altars too. He apparently loved Ireland so much, he wanted his heart to stay there on his death. The little church was steeped in history and a creepy old verger like the ones in Scooby doo cartoons, led them to a vault under the church. He tied back the heavy metal doors, which were on the ground, with chains. Sam said 'Why do you need to do that?' The verger said 'Oh. If you got locked in, it is nearly impossible to open the doors from underneath, because they are so heavy, so we need to chain them up each time!' The vault was dark and cold and there were only two little electric lights in the whole place. It housed, the body of the Irish insurrectionist Robert Emmet, along with the coffins of Bram Stoker's dead relatives, but annoyingly not his. The other end of the crypt had open casks containing an 800year-old nun and the body of a Norman Crusader Knight. It was said that if you touched the fingers of the mummified nun, you would soon come into money. Stan touched the icy bones, but Billy reckoned he would rather stay poor! The verger explained that the atmospheric conditions preserved the bodies in a mummified state. Billy thought the whole place was creepy and was just freaked out by it all. He couldn't wait to get back to the street above. He thought 'I am so like Shaggy in Scooby doo!' He felt great relief when they got back up and the sun shone on his face. The rest of the Dublin visit was just a pub crawl with Billy drinking what seemed like gallons of Coca Cola, as the designated driver. The journey back was quiet, as his drunken mates all slept in the car.

When they eventually got back into Belfast City centre, that evening, there was a slow-moving traffic jam in heavy rain. It was dark by then and because of the rain, Billy struggled to see clearly out of his windscreen. The reason for the hold-up was an army patrol, checking cars. He tried to drive forward at one point and Stan, who was in the passenger seat suddenly woke up from his doze and shouted 'Stop Billy, there's a soldier pointing his gun at you, through the windscreen. Billy hit the anchors and then an angry hand banged on the driver's side window. As he wound down the window, an English accent shouted 'What the fuck are you playing at. I waved you down with a red light! Why did you not stop?' The soldier was so angry, as he had thought Billy had been trying to drive through the checkpoint and was just about to shoot him! Luckily when Billy braked, the soldier realised his error in time. Billy clearly hadn't seen the red light in the rain and the darkness and was a second away from being killed. The soldier carefully checked his ID and his planned destination and after Billy had apologised again for not seeing the red light, they were allowed to go. The soldier was just as shook up as Billy, as he certainly didn't want to shoot an innocent man, but in strife torn Belfast, everyone was living on a knife edge and on another day, this could have had a very bad outcome.

Chapter 12:

Leaving Northern Ireland Behind

There is an old Irish phrase 'Irish mothers and their Sons?' It refers to the fact that Irish mothers are too protective and they 'Mollycoddle' their boys too much. Although Billy was always travelling and basically an independent guy, he usually got homesick if he was away from Belfast too long. He realised that the comforts of home had always held him back from getting out into the real world and taking his life by the horns. During his short time in the Benefits office, he had a life-changing talk with another of his temporary colleagues. She was a part-time singer and a very bubbly character called Susan, who was Assistant Entertainments Manager at Pontin's Holiday Camp in Brean Sands. She only worked there 5 months a year and filled the rest of the year with club singing and temporary jobs, such as the contract they were doing. She was noticeably always happy and this made Billy think about his lifestyle. When she told Billy about the opportunities to sing with resident bands in front of a large audience every night, play sport every day with holiday guests and also teach them things like Archery, French bowls and Volleyball, in beautiful Holiday camp venues; he decided that he needed to apply immediately. This was in January 1988. By February, he had applied to Pontins, giving details of all his music experience in bands and his social and communicative skills as a Trade Union rep. He received a letter shortly after to attend an interview and audition in his beloved Liverpool. Billy had to stay over

in the Britannia Adelphi, where he had previously stayed before Liverpool games and he saw this as a positive omen.

That afternoon he auditioned in an old Working Men's Club in West Derby. The Assistant Entertainments Director from Pontin's who interviewed him, absolutely loved his rendition of Dobie Gray's 'Drift Away' and liked his eccentric outgoing demeanour. A week later he received a letter to attend a Bluecoat training course in Southport, that April.

At the training course, the Bluecoats all learned some standard dance routines and procedures, such as the correct way to greet guests when they arrive at the camps. This also helped them to build up a rapport with each other. Billy struggled with the dancing. He had always had a coordination problem and just felt awkward on the dance floor. He maintained that he preferred to make and create the music and let everyone else dance to him. They also had the obligatory sessions about technical and safety issues. At the end of the three day course, the candidates were put into Bluecoat teams for each of Pontin's 24 camps up and down the country, depending on their particular skills or talents. The Benefits Office job contract finished in early May and neatly fitted with the start of Billy's new job, as a singing Bluecoat on the sunshine island of Jersey. Billy told his Dad at the airport that he wanted to make this a platform for a future singing career, but he was to find that no matter how determined you may be to do something, life always gets in the way and invariably becomes a compromise.

The Pontins camp was in picturesque Plemont Bay, in the St. Ouens' area of Jersey. The perimeter of the island was only a little bigger than the distance of a marathon and he even thought he should try to jog all the way around it sometime. He still had a girlfriend back home, but luckily it wasn't that serious and they had only been together a few months. After his first Bluecoat show in front of an audience of about a thousand, he sent a letter home to her, saying that he wouldn't be back and that he really wanted this to be the start of a new life. The buzz of being on stage felt irresistible to Billy. Within a week he was going out with one of the Receptionists from the camp and suddenly Belfast with all its problems, didn't seem to matter anymore. There were two receptionists in the camp and of course Billy, being a superficial, immature idiot, asked out the tall blonde one, who was called Penny. Within an hour of their conversing, he realised they were chalk and cheese and it wasn't going to go anywhere. The other receptionist was a petite brunette, called Zoe Edwards. Everyone just called her 'Eddie'. He realised he really liked her and they just made each other laugh, all the time. A few days later and after much grovelling from him, she graciously agreed to go out with him.

One of the senior catering staff had heard that Billy did a good Neil Diamond impression. He had imagined him singing 'Love on the Rocks' in his Belfast accent and was horrified at the thought. Zoe had seen Billy and his roommate together and thought they were a comedy duo, so she was also keen to hear him sing. They were very pleasantly surprised that on stage, Billy sang in a mid-Atlantic/American accent and he even sounded a lot like Neil Diamond. The Bluecoat team was an eclectic mix from all over the country and Billy shared a room with a young Comedian, Tommy from Birmingham. The Entertainments manager was a Gay rights campaigner called 'Mario' and his assistant was a transvestite pianist called Jackie from London, who used every opportunity to dress up in the Bluecoat shows. He was a very entertaining pianist also and could play an extensive repertoire of party songs all in the key of 'C', as he bizarrely said that he didn't like the black notes on the piano! There were two pretty girl dancers Lena and Louise from Shropshire, who patiently taught all of the rest of the bluecoats how to waltz, do the old-time dances and all the kids party dances too. There was a female saxophone player, Stacey from Wales, a young lad called Vinny, who looked like a smaller version of one of the brothers from 'Bros' and a young girl singer Justine, who claimed to be 17. She had a powerful voice and was great for the shows, but they found out weeks later, that she was in fact, only 15, still at school and should never have been employed there. She had clearly lied on her application, but she just wanted to learn the stagecraft of singing in front of a crowd every night. They had to let her go, despite the great sound of her voice. Finally, there was another older bluecoat from Yorkshire called Danny. He was originally meant to be Billy's roommate, but the first night Billy walked into his room just after midnight, to find Danny on his bed with a beautiful naked girl bouncing on his manhood. Billy moved to share with Tommy, the very next

day, as he was not going to put up with that every night. Zoe had only had one or two dates with Billy, so it was still a blossoming relationship, but one lunchtime, she came into the dining room to see him scoff a whole bowl of ice cream, in about 30 seconds, right in front of her eyes! It transpired that Mario had put him up to it. Jackie had got the last bowl of ice cream from the kitchen and had to walk the length of the dining room to get a clean spoon. Immediately, the Entertainments Manager said to the blues 'Can someone eat this quickly before he comes back? I want to see the shocked look on his face!' Billy had just finished his own ice cream but, he willingly obliged and for a moment Zoe stared and thought' He's a complete pig! Why am I going out with this guy?'

Every one of the Bluecoats had to take a turn at calling Bingo, which was religiously called at 6pm every evening. Billy had a lot of problems trying to get older ladies, particularly the hearing impaired, to understand his broad Ulster accent, when he called out the Bingo numbers. He had a lot of fun doing the old-time dances with the older lady guests and then there was an exhausting hour every night, dancing with the guests' kids. It was company policy for the Bluecoats to sit and talk and generally mix with the holiday guests every evening, in between duties. They also took turns at being the Pontin's Crocodile, which meant donning the famous six-foot costume and getting battered and kicked by kids for an hour each night. Vinny was the smallest bluecoat and so you could always tell when it was his turn to be the crocodile, because it seemed to have shrunk in size from the night before. The girls were all so ultra-feminine in their mannerisms, that you could always tell when the 'Croc' was a 'Girl' too!

The DJ/Entertainment console was the centre of all the lighting and sound in the main ballroom and so all the

Bluecoats were trained in how to use this. Tommy was a great compere and DJ, as you can imagine for a stand-up comedian. He was in charge of the console and did more 2am finishes than anyone else. It was a very long day for all the entertainment staff, sometimes working 90 plus hours per week, but it was a great way to learn every aspect of the entertainment business. Tommy later in his career became an Entertainments Manager in the Pontin's Blackpool camp and never made it as a comedian, but no one ever forgot his re-creation of his own birth on stage. He only used a Parka jacket as a prop. He had a funny 'Jimmy Cricket' face anyway, but the contorted facial expressions as he squeezed his head through the zipped-up Parka, was one of the funniest things you ever saw.

Tommy and Stacey got on well and they were always coming up with mad ideas to vary the weekly events. On one occasion, the Entertainments Manager took about 30 guests on a nature ramble and Tommy and Stacey both got naked apart from some large, strategically placed docking leaves and a bit of Sellotape. They stood behind a bush, pretending the guests had accidentally wandered into their 'Naturist' camp and they also pretended to be extremely angry. They shouted abusively at the holiday guests, protesting at the invasion of their privacy. The Entertainments Manager played along and appeared to apologise for leading the campers astray. Some of the guests were quite shocked and weren't told until later in the day that they were really bluecoats and that it was all just a wind

up. That was the kind of thing these two liked to get up to. On another afternoon, Billy was leading the Karaoke in the small cocktail bar on camp. Tommy and Stacey decided that anyone singing about water would get soaked and so songs like: 'Raindrops keep Falling on my Head', 'Over the Rainbow' and 'Singing in the Rain' resulted in some very wet bluecoats and quite a few soggy guests! It was great fun, but Billy had to keep the microphones and electrics dry, despite buckets of water everywhere. There was also an occasional 'It's a Knockout!' game based on the old '70s TV show. This involved teams on a small assault course, lots of water and the use of squirty cream, spinning around posts, getting very dizzy. It often ended up like a 1920s slapstick movie. The holiday guests loved it, but were warned not to wear good clothes, before taking part.

Being Irish, Billy was seen as the one person likely to behave aggressively, if anyone took issue with the Blues over anything. He often didn't agree with the strict regime that Mario run and felt that he was constantly picking on the younger Blues. One night after a row with Mario, Billy got a little drunk and kept saying he was going to fetch a bow from the Sports cupboard, go round to Mario's chalet and shoot him with an arrow. He would never have actually done this, but the Restaurant manager got worried about his angry threats and took him back to his chalet instead, to try to calm him down. He gave him more beer and made him smoke a little 'Wacky Baccy'. This not only killed his anger, but left him giggling like a school kid at every single thing people said. This was a totally new experience for him and took the sting out of the situation. The Restaurant manager

was even making light conversation, telling Billy about his recent divorce and how his manipulative ex-wife had taken all his money, while cheating on him for months. The sadder and more depressing this story got, the more Billy chortled. He had never tried 'weed' before or since. The whole incident was never mentioned again.

One week, Billy judged the Glamorous Grandmother competition, along with Tommy. A very attractive, 40year-old blonde lady won it and he presented her with the prize. The problem was, she became obsessed with Billy and wanted to have her wicked way with him in his chalet. She had maybe watched too many 'Carry On' movies and perhaps thought that the male bluecoats were some sort of gigolos, there for her pleasure. Billy was very much in love with his new girlfriend and so this lady's feelings were not reciprocated. He avoided her amorous attention all week and then on the Saturday, which was the traditional leaving day for guests, she came looking for him for a bit of fun, before going home. She had told the other bluecoats what she wanted to do to Billy, so he had to hide himself away. Mario thought this was hilarious and excused Billy from his regular duties for the afternoon. Up until about 3pm that day, Billy was running and hiding in other bluecoat chalets and even nearly fell off a cliff at one point, trying to hide from this lady. Apparently, she was most upset and went home very unhappy about the situation. Phew!! Tommy found Billy sitting on the floor in one of the girl bluecoats chalet's. He was hiding behind the curtains too. 'It's okay Billy, your stalker has gone home!' he laughed. 'Are you absolutely sure?' Billy replied. Tommy grinned, 'Yeah mate, let's go set up for tonight's bingo!'

The Bluecoat job was only seasonal work and so by September, with his girlfriend Zoe in tow. They caught the ferry back to the mainland at Weymouth and began a new life in England. His adventures up to that point, were nothing like the turmoil of living in strife torn Belfast and made him think that he never wanted to live back there again. Billy and Zoe tried several bar and hotel jobs in the next few weeks in Bournemouth and in London, but eventually they decided what they were doing wasn't cost effective with low wages and high rents everywhere they stayed. They had saved up their pennies while 'living in' at Pontin's, but they had had to spend most of these savings in just a few weeks, trying to survive, once they had left that closed environment. They agreed that Billy should try living in the North East and eventually settled in Zoe's native City of Newcastle upon Tyne. Billy had always thought that he would end up living in his beloved Liverpool, but love has a strange way of changing one's intended path. His world was very different now, from the murder and conflict in Northern Ireland. Although life was much better for him, he often felt a deep sadness for the rest of his family and friends, that it would never ever be completely resolved.

Fin.

Printed in Great Britain
by Amazon

60222688R00088